Grace
Makes It Great

by Mary Casanova

★ American Girl®

For Erin Falligant, fine editor, writer, and friend

Published by American Girl Publishing
Copyright © 2015 American Girl

Questions or comments? Call 1-800-845-0005,
visit **americangirl.com**, or write to Customer Service, American Girl,
8400 Fairway Place, Middleton, WI 53562-0497.

Printed in China
15 16 17 18 19 20 21 22 LEO 12 11 10 9 8 7 6 5 4 3 2 1

All American Girl marks, Grace Thomas™, and Girl of the Year® are trademarks of American Girl.

This book is a work of fiction. Any similarity to real persons, living or dead, is coincidental and not intended by American Girl. References to real events, people, or places are used fictitiously. Other names, characters, places, and incidents are the products of imagination.

Illustrations by Sarah Davis

Author photo credit, p. 187: James Hanson

Special thanks to Héloïse Blain, French teacher and language expert, Nice, France; Dawn Bowlus, director, Jacobson Institute for Youth Entrepreneurship at The University of Iowa; Dominique Dury, head chef, Flying Cook, Paris, France; and Donna Houle, special projects manager, Blackstone Valley Tourism Council.

Cataloging-in-Publication Data available from the Library of Congress.

Contents

Chapter 1: A Birthday Wish 1

Chapter 2: Good News, Bad News 17

Chapter 3: Cosmic Cupcakes 33

Chapter 4: On a Roll 43

Chapter 5: The Idea Girl 56

Chapter 6: A Baking Blog 69

Chapter 7: The Great Robot Invasion 81

Chapter 8: For Sale 96

Chapter 9: Dreams of Paris 110

Chapter 10: A Painting Party 125

Chapter 11: Destiny 143

Chapter 12: La Grande Pâtisserie 160

Chapter 13: The Winter Magic Express 170

Glossary of French Words 184

A Birthday Wish

Chapter 1

*F*rom the moment the train conductor called out "All aboard!" to the moment I took my last bite of lunch in the dining car, I'd grinned from ear to ear. Seated across from me, Ella and Maddy smiled back. We rode the slow-moving Bentwick tourist train— creaking, squeaking, clattering, and swaying—along the rails. It was the *perfect* way to celebrate my tenth birthday with my family and friends.

Everything in the train car felt fancy—the dark woodwork, domed ceiling, and lacy valance curtains above white tablecloths. Outside, the valley was a vast green quilt with a few patches of orange and red. The maple trees were just beginning to turn, but in a few weeks, they would be on fire with color. The early-afternoon sun warmed my shoulder as a crisp breeze drifted through the open window.

We passed fields of pumpkins, and orchards where workers on stepladders filled baskets with red apples. Across a pasture, six horses galloped away from us, their heads high and tails outstretched.

When we passed a flock of chickens, Ella exclaimed, "Rhode Island Reds! Just like ours at home!" Her dad had been raising chickens to collect eggs, which we sometimes use for our baking.

Grandpa straightened up in his seat as we wound past the sparkling Blackstone River, carrying canoes and kayaks beneath bridges and through old mill towns. "Y'know, girls," he said, "some of those buildings date back more than two hundred years to the American Industrial Revolution." He nodded toward the stone houses before they disappeared behind us.

Dad's eyes met mine and he gave me a knowing smile. Today, Grandpa was our unofficial tour guide. He knows a lot about Blackstone River Valley history, and Dad and I have heard a lot of it before.

Despite the rocking motion, the server—Grandpa called her a "porter"—managed to carry a cake glowing with candles toward our crowded table. Wearing a black vest over a white blouse, she looked from my friends to me. Her brass name tag read "Destiny," and when she smiled, deep creases appeared around her dark eyes. "September nineteenth. Who's the lucky girl?" She had a thick southern accent, which is unusual here in Massachusetts.

I raised my hand. "Me. But my birthday was actually on the seventeenth." Though taking the Saturday train ride meant waiting a couple of days to celebrate my birthday, it was worth the wait.

"Well, the happiest birthday to you, darlin'!" said Destiny sweetly. "I have never seen such a pretty cake!"

"My grandpa baked it," I explained. "He and my grandma own First Street Family Bakery. But my friends and I bake, too. We started our own baking business."

"Is that so?" Destiny said.

Maddy nodded. "It's called *La Petite Pâtisserie.*"

Destiny looked impressed. "Sounds French."

"It is," Ella added, explaining how we take orders online. "We make *madeleines* and *tartelettes* and other French pastries."

"How elegant! I love to bake, too. I bet it's fun to have your own business," Destiny said enthusiastically.

"I just moved here from Atlanta, and I haven't found a good bakery yet," she explained. "I'll remember all y'all and your French pastries—and I'll look for First Street Family Bakery, too."

When Destiny left, Grandma and Grandpa, Mom, Dad, and Josh broke into song, along with my friends.

". . . Happy Birthday, dear Grace," they all sang, "Happy Birthday to you!"

I smiled at the double-layer white cake trimmed with lavender frosting and aglow with ten flickering candles.

I couldn't believe it was already my birthday. The summer had flown by! On my trip with Mom to Paris to visit Aunt Sophie, I'd dreamed of starting a French baking business. Since then, working together with my friends, we'd launched *La Petite Pâtisserie*—or what we liked to call "LPP." We'd had our first sale at Mom's half marathon in late August and had sold out of everything on our baking cart. Then we set up our own website, and now, two weeks into school, orders were rolling in!

"Are you going to watch the candles melt," Maddy asked, her red hair curled in ringlets, "or make a wish?"

◜ A Birthday Wish ◞

"What are you waiting for, Grace?" Grandpa teased. "Isn't this cake up to your standards?"

Of course it was. It was beautifully decorated, and I knew it would be delicious. Grandpa is an awesome baker. "It's perfect," I said. "I'm just thinking about my wish . . ."

As tiny pools of wax formed at the top of each candle, I decided exactly what I wanted. More than anything else, I wanted *La Petite Pâtisserie* to succeed!

Then I inhaled as much air as my lungs could hold and—with my last ounce of breath—blew out all ten candles.

When the bell rang at the end of the school day on Friday, I headed toward the door where my teacher, Mr. Bauer, was standing. With the weekend ahead, I'd have more time to catch up on baking—and homework.

"Have a cosmic weekend, astronauts!" Mr. Bauer said. Our class was doing a space unit this month, and he wasn't about to let us forget it.

"Roger that!" replied a few students.

Mr. Bauer shook hands with each of us as we left. "And remember, reports due Monday."

"Or we might be shot off into space?" one boy asked.

"In space, anything can happen," Mr. Bauer replied. "Better to always be prepared."

Though I'd had my doubts the first day, Mr. Bauer was turning out to be a pretty fun teacher. All around the room, he'd hung posters of planets and stars, rockets and astronauts. When it was time to clean up around our desks, he would say, "Astronauts, ready your stations!" When we lined up to go somewhere, it was for "our next mission." We weren't just Room 107. We were Apollo 107, with one main objective: "to gain as much knowledge as possible and return home again." And we could address our teacher in one of three ways: "Mr. Bauer," "Captain Bauer," or "Sir." After three weeks, I was catching on to his different style of teaching.

"Grace," Mr. Bauer said when I reached the door. "I hear you bake. Maybe for your report, you'll want to write about what astronauts eat. If you like, you could bake something and bring it to class."

"Yes, sir," I answered with a smile. "Maybe I will."

✑ A Birthday Wish ✑

As I stepped into the hallway, Ella and Maddy were waiting for me.

"How does he know you bake?" Ella asked, her dark hair braided in tiny rows.

I shrugged. "Teachers talk." My mom is a fourth-grade teacher, too, so I figured she'd mentioned my passion for baking to Mr. Bauer.

"Plus," Maddy added, grinning "we advertise. Our baking business isn't exactly a secret."

We quickly stopped by Maddy and Ella's classroom, where Mom shuffled through a pile of papers on her desk. I waved from the door. "Hi, Mom!"

She looked up and smiled. "Hi, Grace. How was your day?"

"It was good," I said. "Meet you at home?"

"Sure thing. See you there, honey!"

Ella and Maddy said good-bye to "Mrs. Thomas," too, and we headed out the front door of the school and found our bikes in the bike rack.

"Mr. Bauer seems really cool and really, really fun," Maddy said.

I felt myself bristle a little. "You mean my mom's not fun?"

Ella rolled her eyes and hooked her arm inside mine. "Of course she is, Grace. Mrs. Thomas—I mean your mom—is also a really nice teacher."

"*I* think she is," I said. Then I sighed. "Honestly, when I first found out that we were in different class-rooms, I felt sorry for myself that you were together in my mom's class and I was stuck in another class. But I'm okay with it now. Mr. Bauer *is* pretty fun."

"Speaking of fun," Maddy said, pulling her bike helmet over her thick red hair, "are we going to bake today?"

"Definitely!" I replied. "Monday, Wednesday, and Friday afternoons," I reminded her. "And Saturdays—at least this month. We have some big orders to fill."

"Got it," she replied.

I glanced sideways at Maddy. It didn't matter if I put our plans on our online calendar. She would still have a hard time remembering to check it. Maddy would never be all that organized, but she brought so many other skills to the table. She created a lot of our advertising. Plus, she helped me remember to keep our business *fun*.

"I still can't believe we're doing it," Ella said,

unlocking her bike. "We're actually running a business together as friends."

"Isn't it great?" I said as I pulled my bike out of the rack. "First it was an idea, and now it's a real business!"

Straddling my bike for a second, I took in the view. Our school sat on the top of the hill above the river. As I looked out across the Blackstone Valley, it reminded me of gazing down on Paris from the high point of *Montmartre*. Everything I had seen—and tasted—in that city had helped me decide what kind of business I wanted to run.

Then I pressed down on the pedal and we cruised downhill toward Bentwick and the winding river below. As I biked after my friends, I realized that we all had had very different reasons for wanting to start *La Petite Pâtisserie*.

For Ella, it seemed mostly about doing something together as friends. Plus, since her dad was still un-employed, she'd wanted to earn some money to help buy her own school supplies, which she did. Now she hopes to help buy her own clothes, too.

Maddy seemed most interested in the art and advertising part of the business. If anything needed to be designed—like our brochures and our website—she was all about it. But mostly, she just liked to be part of anything she considered exciting.

And me? I wanted to see if I could take a hobby I love and launch it into something bigger—into a business I could share with others. I loved the challenge!

As we biked past City-Way supermarket, Maddy piped up. "Hey, y'know how the City-Way bakery always has that promotion of 'Buy one, get one free'?"

"And 'Buy a dozen, get a dozen free,'" Ella added.

As we came to a stoplight, Maddy glanced back at us. "So maybe we need to do something like that?"

Ella wrinkled her nose. "I'm not sure we can afford it," she said hesitantly. Ella is a whiz at math, and she takes care of recording our expenses—whatever we spend on ingredients, supplies, and packaging—as well as what we make in sales. If she thought we couldn't afford a promotion, then we probably couldn't.

"If things were slow," I said, "maybe we'd have to offer a promotion or cut our prices. But right now, we have plenty of orders to fill, don't you think?"

Maddy nodded in agreement. We rode together silently for the last block before arriving at Ella's olive-green house. As Ella turned into her driveway, hens cackled from her backyard.

"I thought they were only supposed to crow in the morning," I said.

"They're not crowing," Ella replied, with a shake of her head. "They're telling us it's time to collect some eggs."

Maddy giggled. "Great! More fresh eggs for us. See you soon, Ella!"

"I'll be over as soon as I can," Ella called over her shoulder as she disappeared into her garage.

Maddy and I continued on to Maddy's white Victorian house. I waited out front while she dashed up the porch steps past the wicker furniture, unlocked her front door, and headed inside with her backpack. In no time, she was back out, her clothes changed, door locked again, and ready to bike with me to my house.

We continued toward home, biking along the dirt towpath beside the canal. From the shallow water below us, a flock of mallards took off, quacking and flapping as they lifted into the air.

When we stepped into my kitchen, we were met by two clashing sounds: Josh's pounding piano chords and Bonbon's whining and barking.

"Josh," I said, glancing into the living room, "you could at least let Bonbon outside when you get home."

My fourteen-year-old brother was bent over the piano in the living room. "I was going to, but I had to get this melody out of my head first," he said, and kept playing.

I exhaled in frustration and headed for the kitchen. I know that Bonbon is my responsibility, but sometimes Josh gets so wrapped up in his music that he doesn't notice anything else.

"How hard is it to let Bonbon outside?" Maddy whispered as she grabbed her apron from the hook in the kitchen.

I shrugged. "Pretty hard, apparently."

With upright ears and big round eyes, Bonbon whined at me from inside her crate.

"Hi, girl," I said, opening her crate door. "Of course you want out. You've been in here all day."

Bonbon tried to run past me, but I held on to her pink collar and steered her toward the backyard. I didn't want her to have an accident on the floor.

"I'll start pulling out ingredients," Maddy called.

"Great!" I called back. We couldn't actually use the oven until Mom got home from school, but we could get going on prep work. Mom would be here soon, anyway.

When I opened the back door, Bonbon tore down the deck steps and out into the yard. She ran in wide circles within the stone wall, yipping excitedly, and then finally stopped and squatted in the grass.

"Good girl!" I praised as I cleaned up after her. Then I found her rope toy and called her to me, and we played a quick game of tug-of-war. I wanted to get back to the kitchen, but I knew Bonbon needed to burn off some more energy. I had an idea.

"Wait here," I said, stepping toward the gate. Mom and Dad had built gates with metal clasps so that Bonbon wouldn't keep escaping through the gaps between the house and the wall.

I pushed through the gate to Mrs. Chatsworth's yard, knocked on the back door, and asked, "Can Zulu come over to play with Bonbon?"

I knew the answer would be yes.

In seconds, I led Zulu, a golden retriever, through the gate to our yard. Bonbon put her head to her paws, her rump in the air. Zulu did the same. And somehow, one of them gave the signal to chase—and they were off, racing around the trunks of the towering oaks and running between Mom's flower beds.

I shook my head, smiling. I love my little dog, but taking care of her sometimes feels like one more thing to juggle along with school and baking.

"Play hard," I called on my way back inside.

While I was washing my hands, Ella showed up, and then the three of us set to work.

Our goal today was to make shells for *tartelettes*—luckily, something we can make ahead of time—so that tomorrow we could fill them with fruit and deliver orders fresh to customers.

"Mr. Williams must have spread the word about our *tartelettes*," I said, using my fingers to fit a round ball of dough into a small *tarte* pan. "I just hope we can keep up!"

Mr. Williams had been our first unhappy customer, but we'd quickly turned him into a big fan of everything we made at *La Petite Pâtisserie*.

Ella looked up from our business notebook, pen and calculator in hand. "Tomorrow, once we make our deliveries, we'll be able to pay ourselves again—maybe fifteen or twenty dollars each."

"Woo-hoo!" Maddy chimed in.

I nodded at the stack of metal pans we'd bought at the Kitchen Shop. "I thought we'd never catch up on spending after we bought all these supplies, but we're making progress! And maybe someday," I said with a sly smile, "we could use our earnings to visit Paris."

Ella laughed. "Yeah, like when we're ninety years old."

Maddy giggled. "I hope it won't take us *that* long to earn enough money. Maybe when we're nineteen?"

I grinned. "It doesn't hurt to dream."

When Mom got home from school, she peeked in on us in the kitchen. She carried a shoulder bag brimming with papers and books.

"Hello, Mrs. Thomas," Ella and Maddy said in unison. They sounded like they were still in Mom's classroom.

"Hi, girls," Mom said. She smiled, but she looked

tired, as she often does at the end of the school week. "Are you ready to use the oven? I'll need to start dinner soon, too."

Over the summer, we'd had all afternoon to bake in the kitchen. Now, we had until five o'clock, which gave us only an hour and a half to work after school—barely enough time to make a mess before we had to start cleaning up again.

"Mom, while you're here," I said, motioning her closer, "we need to check online for orders."

She nodded. "I'll be right there. Let me drop this bag somewhere first. It's heavy."

When she returned to the kitchen, she stood behind us as we gathered around the computer screen. I opened up our website and the screen flashed:

You have 13 new orders!

"Thirteen?" Ella and Maddy screamed with excitement. I was excited, too, but I also had this anxious feeling, like a mini avalanche was heading our way and we were at the bottom of the hill, looking up.

Good News, Bad News
Chapter 2

*I*n two days, we got thirteen more orders?" I said. "That's crazy."

"You mean *exciting*," Maddy said.

I clicked on the order screen to get the details. Many of the orders were for small quantities—from one to two dozen—of *madeleines, tartes,* and *bonbons.* But one order made me suck in my breath.

"Ten and a half dozen *macarons*?" *Macarons* took a really long time to make, especially if we made them in different colors and flavors.

Ella leaned in closer to read the customer's comments aloud: "They need twenty-one boxes with six *macarons* each for a bridal shower."

"By when?" Maddy asked.

"Yikes," I said. "A week from tomorrow!"

"Oh my," Mom said, massaging my shoulders. I was

glad for the weight and warmth of her hands, telling me she understood how big this was for us.

Just then, the doorbell rang. "I'll get it," Mom said. When she returned with Mrs. Eaton, Maddy looked surprised to see her mom.

"Mom! Hi!" Maddy exclaimed. "What's up?"

Mrs. Eaton steered clear of our bowls of batter as she walked through the kitchen. Maybe she was worried that she'd mess up her silky white blouse. Maddy's parents ran an antique shop, and her mom was dressed up in her work clothes.

Mrs. Eaton looked approvingly at the *tartelette* shells that lined the counter. "You girls are doing great work," she said. "It's fun to see you in action!"

"Thanks, Mrs. Eaton," I said.

Maddy was eyeing her mom suspiciously. "What's up, Mom?" she asked again.

Mrs. Eaton slid onto a stool. "Well," she said, "I finally had time to check out residential bakery laws in Massachusetts, as we talked about last month. I learned some good news and some bad news."

"Can you tell us the good news first?" Maddy asked.

"Okay," her mom replied. "The good news is that you girls can apply for a residential bakery license and make *La Petite Pâtisserie* an official business."

Maddy cheered, and Ella and I high-fived.

"We would need to register your business and get a federal tax ID number, and we'd also need to apply for a business certificate through the town clerk," Mrs. Eaton added, "and that's all doable. But there are some expenses involved. The license itself will cost seventy-five dollars."

"Wow," said Ella. I could almost see the math wheels turning in her brain.

Even I knew that we'd have to sell lots of treats to make up for that expense. But if it meant we could be a real business, we should do it. I gave Ella a reassuring smile.

Mrs. Eaton continued. "You would also need to apply for something called a 'ServSafe certification,' which would cost another hundred and thirty dollars."

"Seriously?" I asked, starting to worry now. "A hundred and thirty dollars just to bake out of our own kitchen?"

"Not just to bake, but to bake and sell to the public,"

Mrs. Eaton said. "That's the big difference."

"Goodness," Mom said. "This is all sounding very complicated—and expensive."

"Well, here's the bad news," Mrs. Eaton added. She glanced over at Bonbon's empty crate. "The kitchen will need to be inspected by the public health department. And in licensed residential kitchens, pets need to be kept out of the preparation and storage areas at all times."

My chest tightened as I felt the bad news close in on me like a giant vise. "But Bonbon lives here," I said, my voice coming out wobbly.

Mom gave my shoulder another squeeze. "Don't worry, Grace. Nobody is making Bonbon move out." Then she turned to Mrs. Eaton. "Thanks for doing all this research for the girls. It's clear that there are a lot of rules to follow in order to start a 'real' business. You've given us lots to think about."

Mrs. Eaton nodded. I could tell she felt bad about delivering the not-so-good part of all this news.

"But what are we going to do?" I blurted.

"We're all going to take a deep breath and sit with this information over the weekend," Mom said. "I, for one, am a little too tired to figure it all out right now. Let's discuss this later. Should we talk on Sunday?" She glanced wearily at Maddy's mom.

"Sounds good," Mrs. Eaton replied. "I need to run back to the antique shop, but I wanted to share what I'd found out." She gave us all an encouraging smile. "I know there are some tough hurdles, girls, but if you're really serious about this business, you'll find a way over them."

Mom walked Mrs. Eaton out of the kitchen. They talked quietly together by the front door for several minutes.

My friends and I looked at one another, eyes wide. I glanced at the *tartelette* shells and then back at my friends again.

"What are we going to do, Grace?" Ella asked in a small voice.

"I don't know yet," I said. I sat down at the desk and studied the computer screen. Our thirteen orders were staring me in the face. Could we fill them? Would we even be able to keep our business going?

When Mom returned, she gave us a sympathetic look before slipping on her rubber garden shoes at the back door. Whenever she is stressed, she works outside with her plants. "Don't worry, girls," she said confidently. "I'm sure we'll find a solution." Then, with gardening gloves in hand, she stepped out into the backyard.

I turned back to the computer. Suddenly, Mom was shouting. "Oh no! Zulu! Bonbon! No! Get out of there. Not my mums!"

"Uh-oh," Maddy said, racing to the bay window.

I didn't even want to look.

Suddenly, everything was tumbling together and gathering speed. Between a big order to fill, the bad news about our business, a report due Monday for Mr. Bauer, and Bonbon and Zulu digging where they shouldn't, I felt overwhelmed.

Help!

That night, I tossed and turned so much that I almost rolled Bonbon off the bed. What were we going to do? I couldn't ban Bonbon from the kitchen. That's where we kept her crate! Even if we could pay the extra

fees for running a residential baking business, we'd
need to find another kitchen for baking—a kitchen
without Bonbon. But where?

We couldn't use Ella's house. She had three little
brothers—triplets—who were a tornado in motion.
Her dad was around most days because he still hadn't
found a new job. We needed an adult like him nearby
when we baked, but not a whole swirling family. I
doubted that Mr. and Mrs. Petronia would say yes.

And there was Maddy's house. It was decorated
like something out of a design magazine. I just couldn't
imagine her parents would let us mess up their shiny
kitchen every day. Plus both her parents were always at
their antique shop. Without an adult to help, we weren't
allowed around hot ovens or stove tops. Without an
adult, we weren't even allowed to go online to check
our website for new orders.

When I woke at 7:14, I knew only one thing: I had to
talk with Grandma and Grandpa. They'd been there for
me from the start, encouraging me to do what I love.
They'd been in business for many years. Maybe they
could help me find a way through this new maze of
problems.

I sat up and kissed the top of Bonbon's head. Then I jumped out of bed, and she followed at my heels downstairs to the kitchen.

With a puff of steam, the coffeemaker finished brewing. Dad stood at the stove, flipping French toast with a spatula. Mom sat at the kitchen table, correcting papers.

"Morning," I called over my shoulder as I let Bonbon outside. While Bonbon sniffed around the yard, I scanned yesterday's damage from the deck.

Mom's garden of mums had lost half its flowers. The red wheelbarrow sat beside the flower bed, piled with wilted flowers of burgundy, gold, and amber, their roots exposed and dried out. Bonbon and Zulu had turned digging into a competition. I'd been so busy in the kitchen that I'd failed to check on them in time to stop them. I had promised Mom I'd buy and replant more mums, but she'd waved away my offer, saying, "Grace, thanks, but you have plenty to do."

I clapped my hands together, and Bonbon dashed up the steps to my feet. "Good girl," I said.

When we stepped back inside, I told Mom and Dad that I needed to see my grandparents. "With everything Mrs. Eaton had to say, I want to go ask Grandma and Grandpa for some advice. Can I go over right now and talk with them?"

"After you eat," said Dad, setting plates of French toast on the table beside maple syrup, butter, and glasses of orange juice.

"And remember," Mom said, "it's Saturday morning. They'll have lots of customers."

"I know." I'd helped out at the bakery a lot on weekends and knew that mornings were usually the busiest times.

I ate fast, threw on clothes, and pedaled down to First Street as quickly as I could.

Fortunately, when I stepped inside, there weren't any customers at the counter. I was instantly met by the delicious smells of baked cinnamon and caramel rolls, doughnuts, cakes, and fresh bread. I breathed it all in and smiled.

From behind the swinging door to the kitchen came the sound of guitar strumming—one of Grandpa's country-western stations.

"Ah, here's the sweetest thing in the bakery!" Grandma said, leaving the counter and meeting me on

the other side. She gave me a hug with an extra squeeze
and then looked into my eyes. "I can tell that your busy
mind is working on something this morning, Grace."

I laughed. "You know me better than anyone,
Grandma."

"So what brings you over so early today?" she
asked.

I took in a deep breath. "I wanted to talk with you
and Grandpa. It's about business."

"Sounds serious." Grandma brushed her feathered
bangs back from the edge of her red glasses. "Well, let's
go hunt him down. You're making me very curious."

We stepped into the kitchen filled with white tiles
and stainless steel. Wearing a white apron, Grandpa
was busy pulling baking sheets lined with round
golden loaves from the ovens. "They're old," Grandpa
always said of the two ovens with six rotating shelves.
"But we're keeping 'em. They just don't make ovens
today like they used to!"

"Darling, Grace needs to talk with us," Grandma
called to him.

"Hey-ya, Grace!" he said, turning around and smiling at me. "You're up and at 'em early today."

Good News, Bad News

I poured out my woes about Mrs. Eaton's news, the huge fees we faced licensing our home baking business, and how Bonbon would be banned forever from the kitchen. "Can you imagine that?" I said. "I mean, I wouldn't even be able to bring Bonbon through the kitchen to let her out in the backyard."

"You're a business owner now, Grace," Grandma sympathized. "You have to follow the rules."

It was a compliment to have my business taken seriously, but that didn't make the rules any less frustrating. "Thanks . . . I guess," I mumbled.

"Running a business is a big responsibility, Grace," Grandpa added. "Not only do you have to follow health-department rules, but you need to try to be responsible in other ways, too. For instance, in the early days of industry, folks didn't think much about their trash, and that led to pollution. It took the past few decades and lots of work to clean up the Blackstone River. So all business owners need to follow environmental rules now, too." He pointed toward the recycling bins and the stacks of flattened boxes near the back door. "That's why we separate our trash and recycle all that we can."

I nodded at Grandpa's words, but inside, I was struggling. It was funny to think that the small baking business my friends and I had started might need to follow some of the same rules as this big kitchen. I gazed at the long counters, wide sinks, large mixers, and well-worn baking equipment, and I sighed. "I just wish my friends and I had a real bakery kitchen like this one to use instead of one of our parents' kitchens."

And then a big and really great idea struck.

"Um, I need to ask you two a serious question," I whispered.

"We're all ears," Grandpa said.

I inhaled, looked Grandma and Grandpa in the eyes, and asked, "Is there any possible way that we could use your kitchen—I mean during afternoons and evenings, when you're not as busy? We have lots of new orders coming in, and pretty soon we might not have a place to bake. Could *La Petite Pâtisserie* work here?"

"Goodness," Grandma said, looking around the kitchen as if with new eyes.

My words came out in a rush then. I explained that Maddy and Ella and I could come here after school, pull out our recipes and supplies, and fill our orders.

Good News, Bad News

Grandma and Grandpa listened but said nothing.

"Plus," I said, as if adding a big bonus to my argument, "Mom could have her kitchen back. And she really needs that. It could all work out!" I gave my grandparents my most confident smile and waited for them to respond.

My stomach twisted as I wondered what they would say.

Grandma and Grandpa shared a conversation through their eyes.

My heart beat faster.

"Oh, I just don't know." Grandma gave a slow shake of her head. "First, we'd have to look into guidelines regarding a shared business. And second—" She looked at Grandpa for a long time without saying anything. "Well," she finally said. "Sharing this bakery kitchen just isn't a simple decision right now."

My heart started to sink, but I buoyed it back up. "Grandma, I promise we wouldn't be any trouble. We'd be really careful, and we'd clean up after ourselves, and we'd all be very, very, very responsible."

She kissed the top of my head. "I know you'd do your best, Grace. You always do."

"Tell you what," Grandpa said. "We'll look into it—see if it's something we can try, at least for a while. In the meantime, you girls will need to find an adult who could be here with you after hours, when we've gone home."

An adult who would be with us every moment? It was one thing to have Mom and Dad on call at home if we needed them, but another to have an adult who would stay with us the whole time we were working. That kind of person would be hard to find.

But then I thought of another possibility. "How about Josh?" I suggested.

Grandpa shook his head. "Josh is only fourteen. It's gotta be an adult. No exceptions." He turned to the loaves, loosened them from their pans, and set them to cool on a wire rack.

"How about Mom?" I asked, but even as I said it, I knew the answer.

Grandma smiled. "Grace, your mother is not your Aunt Sophie. She's spent her life trying to get *away* from the bakery business. It's just not her thing. Plus she has her hands full teaching, don't you agree?"

I nodded. My mind was spinning, trying to come

up with a solution. "Dad doesn't get home until after five," I said, thinking aloud. "That's just not early enough to help us out here on weekdays. And he's always doing projects around the house on the weekends, so I don't think he'd have time to help us." My hope began to dwindle.

When the bakery's entry door chimed, Grandma said, "Well, you keep thinking about it, Grace." Then she left to help a customer.

"I will," I said. I glanced at the kitchen clock above the sinks. It was almost nine. "I have to run, Grandpa. My friends and I have orders to fill, and we start in a few minutes."

"Proud of you, Grace," Grandpa said as I gave him a hug good-bye. "I know you're in a hurry, but you haven't branded a loaf in a long time. Maybe that would help you feel better." He nodded toward a rack filled with rising loaves of bread. I knew exactly what he meant, and suddenly my spirits rose, too.

I washed my hands, sprinkled flour lightly on the counter, and grabbed a small chunk of dough from the mixer. Then I quickly rolled out a small ball, used a knife to cut out the letter G, and carefully added it to the top of a round loaf of bread. When the bread came out of the oven, my letter would be part of it, branding it as my own.

"Thanks, Grandpa," I said with a smile. "Now I'll be sure to get my very own loaf." Somehow, working with the dough had cheered me up. "Now I've got to get back to *my* business."

"Thatta girl," he said and waved me off. "Better get going!"

Cosmic Cupcakes
Chapter 3

$\mathcal{W}$hen I arrived home a few minutes late, my friends were already in my kitchen wearing their aprons and adding ingredients to a mixing bowl.

Maddy rolled her eyes and gave me an exaggerated scolding. "Grace, this is why we have everything on a calendar—so people know when to show up."

I glanced at the clock. It was 9:06.

Maddy cracked up. "I'm kidding, Grace. We're fine. Your mom let us in and told us that you went to ask your grandparents for some advice. So?"

"So . . ." I announced grandly, "they might let us use *their* bakery kitchen!"

Ella and Maddy shrieked in response.

"That would be awesome," Ella said. "A real bakery kitchen!"

Maddy agreed. "What a great idea."

"It's not for sure," I quickly added, "because they have to check into more rules, but they said we should think about finding an adult who would be there with us while we work."

I glanced out the bay window at Mom, who was replanting more mums after the dog-digging disaster. "I don't want to ask my mom," I said. "By the time she gets done teaching, she's ready to go home and start dinner—not start supervising us at the bakery."

"My parents are talking about expanding their shop hours," Maddy said. "They both work so much already. If they keep the store open longer, I might as well move in over here."

"Wait," Ella said. "I know! My dad! Until the right job comes along, he might like helping us. He has the time. I could ask, right?"

A thrum of energy went through me. "Your dad? Oh, Ella, that would be perfect! Can you call and ask right now?"

She shook her head. "He's at a karate demonstration with the three E's." The three E's were Ella's triplet brothers, named Ernie, Eddy, and Eino.

"Could you text him?" I asked. I didn't want to be

pushy, but the sooner we had a plan in place, the sooner I could breathe again.

"Sure!" Ella took out her phone and tapped a quick message to her dad.

I wanted to stare at Ella's phone and will her father to respond quickly, but we had to turn back to our orders, which were staring at us from the computer screen. It was hard to know how to manage so much work at once. We had to get organized.

I had an idea.

I dashed outside to where Mom was working in her garden, and I asked her about the poster board she kept on hand in the laundry room.

"Sure," Mom said when I told her my plan. "Great idea, honey," she called after me as I raced inside.

I laid a sheet of poster board on the kitchen table. With a marker, I made one huge calendar. I turned to the computer and copied each order onto the board, under the day of the week it was supposed to be delivered. Then I worked backward to figure out our baking schedule so that our products would be fresh for delivery. Some things could be made ahead of time and frozen, but not everything.

Then I taped the board up on the pantry door, where we could all easily see it.

"Wow," Maddy said. "That's great. It breaks a huge mountain down into small hills. We can do this, can't we?"

I nodded. "We'll tackle these orders, and then after our deliveries next Saturday, maybe, with a little luck, we'll move our business over to the kitchen of First Street Family Bakery."

"I hope so!" Maddy said.

"Are your grandparents charging us anything to use their space?" Ella asked.

I paused. I hadn't thought of that. "I don't know," I said. "I guess we'll have to wait and see what they say. But for now, we'd better get busy baking," I said with renewed energy.

Just then, Ella's cell phone dinged. "It's my dad," Ella said. "And he says, 'Sounds like fun. Count me in!'"

We did a quick dance and cheer session around the kitchen, and then we forced ourselves to settle down and get to work—filling one order at a time.

Cosmic Cupcakes

Mom wasn't happy that I'd put off my report on astronaut food until Sunday night, especially when she found out that part of the report involved baking. "Oh, Grace. It's eight o'clock, you've been pushing hard all weekend, and now you're going to squeeze in a report *and* start baking at this hour?"

I felt a little bit like Bonbon getting scolded after misbehaving. "It's okay, Mom," I said quickly. "I've already done all the research for the report, and I picked one of Grandma's super-easy recipes. While the cupcakes are baking, I'll write my paper. It'll go fast."

Mom sighed. She filled the teakettle with water and put it on the back burner. "I'll be in the living room," she said when her tea was ready. "Let me know when you need the oven."

It wasn't that I *had* to bring a treat as part of the assignment, but I had it in my head that it would be more fun if I did. Unfortunately, by the time I was all done with my report and with cleaning up the kitchen, it was after ten o'clock. I felt as tired as I did the day Mom and I flew home from Paris.

As I turned off the kitchen lights and woke Bonbon to follow me upstairs, Mom said, "Grace, sweetie, I know this weekend was an exception. You had lots you needed to do, but no more late nights like this, okay? Schoolwork has to come before your bakery business."

I nodded. "Okay. Thanks for staying up with me, Mom." I wrapped my arms around her waist. "Good night."

Mom kissed the top of my head. "Good night, my little baker."

I smiled at that. I was tired, but also excited because I'd found a way to combine baking and schoolwork. I couldn't wait to share my "tasty" report with my classmates tomorrow!

The next morning, I was still tired—but ready. I stood at the front of the class, a little jittery to have everyone's eyes on me. I cleared my throat, and then read aloud from my report:

What Astronauts Eat

In early space missions, gravity caused all kinds of prob-

❧ Cosmic Cupcakes ❧

lems with crumbs and liquids flying around, so astronauts
ate meals from squeeze tubes. Of course, the food wasn't very
appealing. I mean, who wants to eat a meal out of a tube?
Plus, astronauts couldn't bring fresh fruits and vegetables on
board, because they wouldn't last very long in space. So it
was hard to bring tasty, healthy meals, and it didn't take long
before space travelers were losing too much weight.

That's why many astronauts began to eat freeze-dried
foods, which keep for a long time. All they have to do is add
water to the dried foods at a rehydration station on the space
shuttle.

Today, in the International Space Station, or ISS, one of
the favorite items on the menu is freeze-dried shrimp cocktail
with horseradish-infused powdered sauce! Astronauts can eat
freeze-dried anything, from steak to chocolate cake.

When I finished reading, I turned to the supply
cupboard and pulled out the baking box I'd stashed
before class.

"Because we're studying space and astronauts,"
I said, "I brought a space treat: Cosmic Cupcakes."

Mr. Bauer led the class in a round of applause as
I began handing out the cupcakes.

"With chocolate frosting," a girl named Amelia said. "My favorite!"

A boy named Marcos raised his hand and asked, "So these were freeze-dried? You just added water and they turned into cupcakes?"

I laughed. "Maybe that works up in space, but here on earth, I made them the old-fashioned way."

Another girl, whose name was Brooke, said, "You mean, you used a box of cake mix?"

"I know lots of people make cupcakes that way," I said, "but I like to bake from scratch."

Mr. Bauer said, "Grace, you might explain what you mean."

"Oh, right, that means I don't use premade mixes. I start with flour, sugar, and whatever else the recipe calls for. Sometimes I add my own ingredients, too. I love to bake. My friends and I started a business called *La Petite Pâtisserie,* and we sell our own French pastries."

Mr. Bauer let everyone chat as we ate our cupcakes. As I took a bite of mine, I worried that I might have said too much. But then another girl raised her hand and asked, "Where can I get some of the French treats?"

I grinned and told her the website address for
La Petite Pâtisserie. Mr. Bauer nodded approvingly,
and I could feel my cheeks flush. I'd done well on my
report. My classmates liked my cupcakes. And I'd even
managed to advertise my business!

The rest of the school day was a bit of a blur. I got
really tired listening to everyone's space reports. At
some point during the math lesson in the afternoon,
I felt a *tap-tap* at the back of my head. "Grace?"

I blinked, unsure of where I was. I'd been dreaming about giant vats of batter and of orders coming in
so fast that our printer was spitting them out—and my
friends and I were getting buried in paper.

"*Psst!* Grace," the voice came again.

It was Marcos, who sat behind me.

I blinked my eyes open and spun around.

Marcos held up the eraser end of his pencil, which
he pointed toward the front of the room. "Captain
Bauer asked you a question," he whispered.

"Grace?" Mr. Bauer asked. "Are you unwell?"

A twitter of giggles rose up around me.

"Do you need to go to the nurse's office?"

I couldn't believe it—I'd fallen asleep in class! I gazed at all the math problems Mr. Bauer had written on the board. Which one was he asking about?

"Um, what was the question?" I mumbled. But before he could answer, I shook my head. "Never mind. I won't know the answer. I fell asleep," I admitted.

Luckily, Mr. Bauer wasn't angry. "Make sure you get enough sleep tonight so you can be more alert in class tomorrow, yes?" he said.

"Yes, sir," I answered, my face burning hot with em-barrassment. Mom had been right about my late-night baking. I should have started earlier. I fought another yawn and sat up straight. I had to stay awake for the rest of the day.

On a Roll

Chapter 4

On Saturday, with help from Ella's dad, we drove our huge order of *macarons* to the Red Goose Inn, a bed-and-breakfast on the outskirts of Bentwick. The driveway curved through flaming maples and stopped at a small parking lot packed full with cars.

"Do you want me to go with you?" Mr. Petronia asked as we jumped out of the backseat.

"No, we've got it," Ella said.

"Thanks anyway," Maddy added.

Ella, Maddy, and I carried three big boxes to the towering brick house. The front steps were decorated with pumpkins and gourds and looked ready for trick-or-treaters.

I tapped the door's steel knocker: a goose painted cherry red. When the door opened, a tall woman with cropped hair greeted us.

"Ms. Dodd?" I asked.

She glanced at our boxes, labeled with our business logo and name. Then she looked toward Mr. Petronia's car. "Are you delivering these for your parents?" she asked.

"I'm Grace," I said, forcing a smile. "And this is Ella and Maddy. *La Petite Pâtisserie* is *our* business. It says so right on our website."

"Mmm-hmm," Ms. Dodd said. "I ordered through the website. I guess I didn't read the fine print. But I have a party here that requested *macarons*—the *real* French version. I bake, but I wasn't going to pretend to be an expert at something like that. Oh dear."

She frowned, as if the fact that we were kids meant our products would be a huge disappointment. "Well, I'd better take a look," she said. "They have to be authentic *macarons*. Otherwise I can't accept them."

My stomach dropped. We'd slaved to finish this huge order on time. Ella and Maddy had arrived at my house extra early this morning, and we had carefully packed the assorted flavors and colors of *macarons* six to a box, just as Ms. Dodd had requested. We had centered our *La Petite Pâtisserie* logo stickers on the top of each package, with our contact information and all of our ingredients listed, just as Grandma and Grandpa had taught us. We had worked so hard to make everything perfect, but what if Ms. Dodd didn't agree?

As she reached out to open the lid of the large box in my hands, I suddenly flashed back to one of the first deliveries we'd ever made. We'd ridden our bikes to Mr. Williams's house with a box of *tartes* in my bike trailer. When we delivered the box, the *tartes* were all broken into pieces because the bike path had been so bumpy. Mr. Williams had been very upset. We had made things right by delivering a fresh and unbroken batch, but I would always remember the feeling of embarrassment when Mr. Williams was unhappy with our product.

I didn't know if Ms. Dodd would be happy with our *macarons*, but at least I could make sure none of them were broken before she looked at them. "Let me set the box down so you can take a look," I suggested. "I don't want to drop them."

I walked to a table on the porch and carefully set down the box.

"Well, your packaging is lovely," said Ms. Dodd.

"A French bulldog. Very cute."

"Thank you," Maddy answered proudly. She was the one who had designed the logo.

As Ms. Dodd opened the big box and then one of the smaller boxes within, I held my breath. The perfectly round cookies in pink, light green, yellow, and orange looked as beautiful as any I'd seen in the window cases in France. But would that satisfy Ms. Dodd?

"They certainly are pretty!" she said.

"I learned how to bake these in Paris," I blurted. "Now my friends and I make them here."

The woman's eyes widened. "Paris? Is that right?"

"My aunt and uncle run their own *pâtisserie* there," I added. Once I started explaining, my words tumbled out like falling autumn leaves. "If we run into any trouble, we get help from our French consultant." I didn't mention that our "consultant" was my younger cousin, Sylvie—my Aunt Sophie's stepdaughter.

"Well, is that so? I just never dreamed that such young girls could run such a professional business." She nodded and carefully closed up the boxes. "I'm willing to try these *macarons*. If my guests like them, I may order more. Bring them into the kitchen, please. I'll write you a check."

Maddy, Ella, and I looked at one another with relief—and pride.

When we finished all our deliveries, Mr. Petronia dropped us off at my house. It was mid-afternoon, and Ella and Maddy and I had planned to relax by going biking. Then we were going to get Bonbon and Maddy's dog, Murphy, together for a playdate.

But when we arrived home, a silver car was parked in our driveway. "That's my grandparents' car," I said.

"Do you think they have an answer for us about using their kitchen?" Ella asked.

I nodded. "Cross your fingers," I whispered nervously to my friends as I opened the front door.

We found Mom and Dad and my grandparents on the deck out back, sipping coffee. Bonbon ran out from under the table, and I scooped her up in my arms. Her smooth little tongue immediately found my cheek.

Before I could say a word, Grandpa gave me an

exaggerated wink and a nod.

"We can?" I blurted. "Oh my gosh!"

Maddy bounced on the balls of her feet. "Really?"

"That's awesome!" Ella added.

Grandma put up her forefinger. "Wait, girls. There's a catch. We looked into the rules and learned that in order to share our kitchen with you, you'll still need to apply for a business license. And your grandpa and I will need to apply for a 'commissary kitchen license,' which is quite expensive."

"How expensive?" Ella asked, sitting down.

"Three hundred dollars," Grandma said. "We might be able to help a little with it, but—"

"No, Mom," my own mother interrupted. "That's not your responsibility."

"Three hundred?" I repeated, closing my eyes. I buried my face in Bonbon's warm fur. Why did every step forward feel so hard? I felt like someone out there wanted us to fail, to quit following our dream. We were starting to make a little money at our baking business, but nothing close to three hundred dollars.

When I looked up, Mom gave me a sympathetic smile. "Here's what I think. Your dad and I could pay the fees for the licenses and invest in your business. We'd lend the money to you, and then you girls could pay us back as your business grows."

"But what if it doesn't grow?" I said, my voice breaking. "What if we can't pay you back?"

"Then we'll have made a poor investment," she said, looking to Dad, who nodded in reply.

"But," Dad added, "we think your business is going to do just fine."

I swallowed hard. Then I looked from Ella to Maddy. "What do you think?" I asked them.

Maddy beamed. "I think we're on a roll!"

Ella just grinned.

I glanced back at Mom and Dad, their eyes full of belief in me—in the business I'd started with my friends. I gave each of our "investors" a giant hug.

It would take a couple of weeks to get the licenses we needed, but that didn't mean we couldn't start moving! We were so excited that instead of biking that afternoon, we packed up our baking supplies from my house. Mr. Petronia drove over in his minivan, and we filled it with packaging supplies, French baking cookbooks, and all the equipment we had bought. While we packed, we talked about how excited we were to use the equipment in Grandma and Grandpa's kitchen— especially for larger orders. Then we squeezed into the van and headed to First Street Family Bakery.

Grandma and Grandpa were waiting there to help us get settled in and organized. While we had been packing up at my house, they had cleared off several shelves and one long countertop for us to use, as well as a couple of shelves in one of their refrigerators.

Grandpa gave us a tour, covering everything from proper hand washing at the sinks, to the location of fire extinguishers, to special oven instructions for Mr. Petronia.

"The ovens each have six rotating shelves, which helps everything bake evenly," Grandpa explained. "They're over sixty years old. Heck, they're antiques, like me." Grandpa winked at me. "But if they ain't broke, I say, don't fix 'em."

Grandma chuckled. "See why I had such a battle trying to get him to agree to buy a laptop? He's an old turtle sometimes." Then she turned to us. "Girls, there's nothing like learning by doing. So why don't you go ahead and whip up something—maybe a new recipe— just for fun? We'll stick around to answer any questions that come up."

As we put on our aprons, I glanced back at my grandparents, who for the first time in forever were sitting down in their kitchen. I have so many good memories of hanging out with them here, but they were always bustling around the room, making half a dozen different things at once. I'd always thought I was such a big help to them, stirring a bit of batter or punching down a bowl of yeasty dough. Now that I know how much work actually goes into baking, I realize how hard my grandparents have worked all these years. Somehow, they've always made it seem easy. Grandma and Grandpa are experts at what they do. Maybe it's because they love baking—just like me.

I pulled my tablet from my backpack and said, "We like to play French music to put us in a French baking mood. Do you mind if we play some here?"

"What, instead of my country music?" Grandpa made an exaggerated frown. Then he started singing a few bars of a twangy song about a cowboy.

Grandma wagged her head. "Honey, not everyone loves country the way you do. Don't torture the girls."

"French music?" Grandpa said. "Well, why not? Looks like I'm in *your* kitchen at the moment, Grace."

I grinned at him. Then, as French folk songs floated around the bakery, I looked at the blinding white walls surrounding us on every side.

"Would you mind one more thing?" I asked.

"What's that, Grace?" Grandma tilted her head at me, smiling in a way that told me she was proud of me and happy to help us out.

"Sometime, could we put up a few French posters? Maybe on just one wall, to help keep us inspired?"

"*Mais oui,*" Grandma replied.

"But yes?" I translated. "Grandma, I didn't know you knew French!"

"A little," she said. "After all, our daughter and her husband—and now two of our granddaughters— speak French. I really should learn the language. Will you help me practice?"

"*Bien sûr!* Of course!" I said.

I turned to Maddy and Ella. "Let's try a different

flavor of *macarons*—something that reminds us of fall," I suggested. *Macarons* were one of our customers' favorites, and it was fun to try new flavors.

"Like what?" Maddy asked.

I already had an idea up my sleeve. "Like pumpkin-cinnamon!"

Ella nodded. "Yum. I love anything with pumpkin."

Grandma and Grandpa told us we could use some of their ingredients, such as flour, baking soda, sugar, and other dry goods.

As we worked, Maddy brought up the conversation we'd started last week. "I still think we should all go together to France someday."

"We could hang out with my cousins Sylvie and Lily," I added, catching her enthusiasm.

"A trip like that would cost a fortune," Ella said realistically. "Maybe we could afford it in twenty years."

"Why not dream about it?" I asked. "We could make it a reality. We dreamed of starting a business, and now we're doing it."

"It doesn't cost anything to dream," Grandpa agreed.

I glanced over at him. "Everything starts with an

idea, right, Grandma and Grandpa? Like your bakery?"

They both nodded and smiled at us, but there was a hint of sadness in their faces. Maybe they were just remembering back to when they'd first started the bakery—and now they felt wistful.

Wistful. It was a word I'd learned in one of Mom's teacher moments. We'd been sorting through clothes I'd outgrown and bagging them up to donate to charity.

"Oh, look," Mom had said, holding up a green velvet holiday dress that I'd worn when I was little. "You looked so darling in this outfit, and you loved wearing it. Seeing this again makes me wistful."

When I'd asked what the word meant, she'd said, "The only thing separating _wishful_ and _wistful_ is a single letter. _Wishful_ means feeling hopeful for something and looking to the future. _Wistful_ is feeling sadness about something and longing for the past."

Sitting side by side on their stools, Grandpa put his arm around Grandma's shoulder and pulled her closer. She leaned into him. They seemed _wistful. Why?_ I wondered. Could they be thinking about all the moments in the bakery they'd shared over the years?

That made me think of the trip I wanted to take to

On a Roll

France with my friends someday.

And that definitely made me feel *wishful*.

The Idea Girl

Chapter 5

*B*ecause I'd been so busy with LPP, I hadn't had time to video-chat with Sylvie. We usually did it on Sundays at noon Massachusetts time, which meant six p.m. in Paris. It was a good way for us to stay close. Plus, as my "business consultant," Sylvie wanted to hear all about our orders and what we were baking. As I turned on my computer, I realized how much I'd missed talking with her.

From the screen, Sylvie peered back at me with her big brown eyes. In her arms, she cradled her golden tabby, Napoléon. "How are you, Grace?" Sylvie asked in English.

I wanted to say, "Me? I'm fine," but I had to think for a moment in order to translate it into French. *"Moi? Je vais bien,"* I replied. And then I returned her question. *"Comment vas-tu?"*

"Me? I'm fine, too," she answered. I could tell right away that she'd been working on her English. She could practice every day with her parents.

I nodded and smiled. I wanted to ask how baby Lily was, but my brain churned, trying to form the right words. I could feel my French already slipping away. *"Comment vas-tu?"*

Sylvie laughed lightly. "Me? I'm still fine," she replied.

I shook my head. *"Pardonne-moi,"* I said. *"Comment famille?"*

"Comment va ta famille?" she gently corrected.

"Oui," I said, feeling a little flustered. *"Merci."*

"My family is fine," she said. "My mom, my dad, my baby sister. All fine." Then she rattled off something long and fast in French, and I figured from her expression that it had something to do with being frustrated by our language differences.

"I miss you!" I said, pantomiming that I'd hug her if I could.

She put her fingers to her lips and blew me a kiss. *"Je t'aime!"*

Then Aunt Sophie appeared with baby Lily, whose

cheeks had filled out and whose dark hair was tied in a tiny pink bow at the top of her head.

"Hi, Aunt Sophie! Hi, Lily!" I exclaimed.

Lily wiggled in my aunt's arms. I liked to think that she still recognized the sound of my voice.

"Aunt Sophie," I said, "please tell Sylvie that my friends and I are dreaming of coming to France someday. Our business is really taking off!"

"Yes, so much so," Mom said, coming up behind me, "that they've moved from my kitchen to First Street Family Bakery's kitchen in the late afternoons."

"Congratulations, Grace!" Aunt Sophie said.

"So we're dreaming bigger," I added. "Please tell Sylvie for me."

Aunt Sophie translated, and Sylvie moved in closer. Her face appeared bigger on the screen, and she was grinning. *"C'est génial!"*

Then it was time to log off. Sylvie said, "Good-bye, Grace."

"Au revoir, Sylvie," I answered before the screen went blank.

I turned to Bonbon at my feet. "C'mon, girl," I said, grabbing her leash and clipping it to her collar. "Time for a walk." Because the backyard was enclosed and Bonbon couldn't escape, I usually just opened the back door and let her out. But I knew she loved our walks, too, so I tried to fit one in every afternoon.

Nose to the ground, Bonbon snuffled and snorted as we walked the towpath alongside the canal, where half a dozen Canada geese floated. When one honked, Bonbon started yapping. One of the geese lifted its head higher, at full alert, watching us carefully until we'd passed.

"You don't want to try to take them on," I assured Bonbon.

Dry leaves swished around our feet. Red squirrels and gray squirrels dashed up and down tree trunks, carrying their stash and hiding it who-knows-where. With every sighting of a squirrel, Bonbon tugged a little at the end of her leash, ready to chase. I had to call her back so that she would remember to walk quietly beside me.

"You have to walk nice, Bonbon," I said. "You know how." I was learning how to train Bonbon, and she was doing well.

I breathed in the spicy air and the tang of turning

leaves. In open stretches, the sun warmed my face, but in the shadows of trees, I felt a slight chill. The days were getting shorter now, which reminded me that Halloween was coming soon.

Last Friday, on top of giving us homework in math and reading, Captain Bauer had announced, "I want you to find a box and start working on your robot project for Halloween." As part of our science and technology unit this month, he wanted us to dress up as robots to prepare for what he called "the Great Robot Invasion" at our school.

"A robot," I said to Bonbon as we walked, "is not exactly my dream costume, but it looks like I'll have to come up with something."

She glanced up and whined at me, as if she understood perfectly.

When we returned home, I headed to the garage where Josh was rebuilding a bike. "Help!" I said. I told him about the robot assignment and asked if he had any suggestions.

"Well, you probably don't have tons of time to make the costume, right?" he asked, adjusting the tension on the hand brakes.

"That's for sure," I said. "There's Bonbon to take care of, baking orders to fill and deliver, and homework on top of it all."

"Well, for starters," he said, leaning over the handlebars, "the robot costume doesn't have to be a lot of work. Just find a big box, cut holes in the sides for your arms and one on top for your head, and spray-paint it with metallic paint."

"But won't the costume need some gadgets and wiring?" I asked. I looked around at all of Josh's extra bike parts, which were sorted and organized in plastic bins. "Could I use some of these bike parts? I could glue them on, couldn't I?"

Josh saw what I was eyeing and shook his head vigorously. "This all may look like junk to you, Grace, but I actually need this stuff. Besides, why not make the robot something more *you*?"

"More me?"

He nodded. "You're the idea girl. You'll figure it out."

"Thanks," I said, though my head felt full of rocks. I was fresh out of ideas.

After dinner, I climbed onto the cushions in the bay window with my backpack. Bonbon hopped up beside me. It helped that she liked to keep me company while I did my homework. First, I did my math problems. When I turned to my reading assignment, Bonbon peered out the window, watching for squirrels even though it was too dark to see.

I pressed my head gently against hers and stared out the window, too. When I heard the wind rustling through the trees, I thought again about my Halloween costume. I still couldn't see how to make my robot more *me*.

"Maybe coming up with good ideas is like looking for squirrels," I whispered into Bonbon's ear. "Maybe, sometimes, all we can do is watch and wait."

Two weeks later, our business license arrived. My grandparents' kitchen had been inspected and approved as a commissary kitchen, so LPP was officially back in business!

On Monday, my friends and I met at First Street Family Bakery to fill our first orders in our new space. Instead of heading home, Grandma and Grandpa stayed with us. They seemed happy to sit and just hang out for a while.

"Do you mind if we put up a whiteboard?" I asked them. We'd bought an inexpensive one, along with a set of colorful markers.

"Go right ahead," Grandpa said. "Put it somewhere where it's easy for you girls to get at it."

Mr. Petronia—or "Mr. P.," as we'd started to call him—helped us hang the board near the swinging door that led to the front of the bakery. "If the job doesn't get on the board," he said to Grandpa over his shoulder, "it doesn't get done."

"So true!" I agreed.

Maddy nudged me and nodded toward the folder in her hands. She had come armed with images of Paris that she'd found online: a *pâtisserie*, bakery treats, statues, the Eiffel Tower, a woman carrying a *baguette*, a fountain, and a man walking three small dogs on leashes.

"Oh, that's right. Grandma, we brought some pictures of Paris, too," I said.

"Go right ahead and put those up, too," she said.

As Maddy and Ella taped up images, I said,

"I almost feel like I'm back in Paris!"

"I know. It makes me want to go there even more," Maddy said, climbing the step stool and posting a photo of colorful *macarons*.

Once the atmosphere was set, we settled into our routine. First we checked our website for new orders. Ella read the orders aloud and I wrote each one—and the delivery date—on the whiteboard. Then we washed our hands, donned aprons, and got to work.

Mr. P. seemed more than happy to help us with today's new recipe: mini cream puffs. And Grandpa jumped in with a suggestion or two while we worked.

"While you're baking the shells," he said, "put the heavy cream in the freezer for a bit. Make sure it's extra cold before you start. The cream will whip up faster, and you'll get the light, fluffy texture you want."

I beamed at him. There's that old expression about "too many cooks in the kitchen" being a bad thing, but today, I felt like "many cooks in the kitchen" couldn't be better.

In what seemed like no time at all, we'd baked dozens of shells. While the shells cooled, we made the whipped cream and divided the batch into two smaller bowls. One would become chocolate cream and the other, vanilla cream.

"If these work, I want to try them in a bunch of flavors," I said, slicing open a puffy, hollow shell and spooning a dollop of filling in the middle. "The recipe said we could make hazelnut, pistachio, coffee, and raspberry cream."

"But how do we know which ones customers are going to like the most?" Ella asked. "What if we make a bunch of pistachio cream puffs and no one buys them? We'd have to dump them—and we'd lose money."

"I'm happy to taste-test them all for you girls," Grandma joked.

I giggled, but there was a seed of an idea in Grandma's words. "Maybe we *should* do some taste testing with customers," I turned to Grandma. "How could we make that happen?"

"What do you girls think?" Grandma asked, looking at me and Ella and Maddy.

We were all quiet, deep in thought, as we continued filling cream puffs.

"From the cart!" Maddy said suddenly.

The moment she said the words, I could see it: our

beautiful cart with an assortment of mini cream puffs in a bunch of different flavors. "That's it!" I said. "We can set it up just outside on First Street. We can give away free samples."

"Free?" Ella said, her eyes doubtful.

"Free," I repeated. "That way customers will feel *free* to tell us which ones they like best. Then we'll know which ones to make more of."

"And," Maddy said, "we can have them write reviews as they sample the different flavors. The more good reviews, the better!"

Grandpa nodded his approval. "Good thinking, girls. Samples and reviews make good business sense."

While we cleaned up, we made plans to meet again on Wednesday and bake more mini cream puffs as well as *macarons* in some fun new flavors. And on Friday, we'd display our cart outside the bakery and do a taste test. I couldn't wait!

Maddy handed each of us a small box of the mini cream puffs we had made today. "Don't forget to get reviews at home, too," she said. "We need good ones before we can add cream puffs to our menu."

Grandma smiled at the box in her hand. "These are

coming with me to my book club tonight." Then she checked her watch and added, "Oh dear. I'm going to miss it altogether if I don't get going! See you girls on Wednesday."

"Thanks, Grandma," I said. "You're the best."

She winked at me as she followed Grandpa out the door.

As I closed the door behind them, I noticed the stack of large empty boxes near the recyclables bin. "Woo-hoo!" I exclaimed.

"What?" Maddy asked.

"What did you find?" Ella joined in.

I pointed to the stack of cardboard boxes.

Ella's eyebrows scrunched together. "I don't get it. What's so exciting about boxes?"

"Nothing," I said, "unless you're supposed to make a robot costume for Halloween and the first step is finding a big box. Then this is a gold mine!"

"You get to make robots in Mr. Bauer's class?" Ella asked.

I nodded. "I think our whole class might parade around school. Mr. Bauer is calling it the Great Robot Invasion."

"Oh, that sounds soooo fun!" Maddy whined. "We're not doing that in—" She stopped short.

I had a sinking feeling. "My mom's class," I finished for her. I shrugged. "I can't help it that Captain Bauer comes up with all these crazy ideas."

"Actually," Ella said, "did you know we're decorating our classroom for Halloween?"

"You are?" I said. "My mom hasn't said a thing about it."

Ella clamped her hand over her mouth. "Maybe it's supposed to be a surprise," she said in a muffled voice. "Just like your robot invasion."

I pretended to lock my lips and throw away the key. Then Maddy and Ella did the same.

A Baking Blog
Chapter 6

*O*ur bakery cart was a magnet.

The moment we pushed it out onto the sidewalk in front of First Street Family Bakery, people stopped to investigate.

"Free samples," we called to walkers and bikers. And nearly every time, they stopped to sample our new flavors of mini cream puffs and *macarons*.

"Yum!"

"Delicious!"

"Incredible!" came the responses.

And we were quick to pull out a notepad and pencil. "Would you mind writing a quick review?" we would ask.

It didn't take long to see which flavors were the most popular. Our pumpkin-cinnamon *macarons* were a big hit, along with the raspberry cream puffs.

"Now we know which ones to bake more of," Ella said.

"Exactly," I replied.

Even Mr. Hammond from the Kitchen Shop dropped by. "It's just amazing what you girls have accomplished!" he exclaimed. "My customers rave about what they order from you. I hope you're having fun, too. Are you?"

I beamed. I couldn't imagine anywhere else I'd rather be than outside my grandparents' bakery, in the shade of a fuchsia-leaved maple tree, working the LPP bakery cart with my friends. "It's lots of work," I admitted to Mr. Hammond, "but we're having a blast."

He smiled and nodded. "Good to hear. Even though it's work, I love running my shop and being in business for myself. There's always something new to learn, like the blog I started a few months ago." He ran his hand through his short-cropped hair. "That was a bear. I had no idea what I was doing at first with it, but after a while, it came as natural as breathing."

I like talking with Mr. Hammond. He treats us like real business owners—which we are!—and sometimes gives us good ideas, too.

A Baking Blog

In fact, the moment he walked out of earshot, Maddy's eyes lit up. "Ella. Grace. We need a blog!"

Ella made a face. "With school and all, I don't see how we can add another thing to LPP." Ella was good at being practical and making sure we didn't get in over our heads.

But I couldn't help getting excited about Maddy's idea. "Like the blog I had in Paris?" I asked. I had started a blog on my mom's teacher site, and it had been a fun way to stay in touch with Maddy and Ella back home.

"Exactly," Maddy answered. "A blog is a great way to advertise and get people excited about our business. Between our website, our taste tests, and a blog, our business can grow—and grow—and grow." With each *grow* she extended her arms wider, until she knocked our "Free Samples" sign off the top of our cart. "Oops!"

Ella picked up the sign and immediately rehung it.

"Thanks," said Maddy, but she'd lost none of her enthusiasm when she asked me, "Could we put our blog on your mom's teacher site again, like you did when you were in France?"

I took a deep breath. "Maybe . . ." I said, "but she

won't have time to help with it like she did during the summer."

"Wait!" Ella finally joined in. "My dad might be able to help us with that. Let's ask him this afternoon."

Yes!

And with that, another good idea was launched.

When we asked Mr. P. what he thought of our blog idea, he was sitting on a stool in the bakery kitchen, sampling one of our new mocha *macarons*. "Mmm, this really is delicious," he said, wiping the crumbs from his lap.

"Dad!" Ella sighed impatiently. "What do you think of the *blog*?"

Mr. P. nodded enthusiastically. "I think a blog is a fine idea. I'd be happy to help supervise it—as long as you girls write the posts and take the photos. You're the experts, after all." He winked.

"Oh, good!" I said.

Ella grinned. "Thanks, Dad."

Maddy pulled out her cell phone. "Mr. P., would

you hold up a mocha *macaron* and smile, please?"

Click!

"It can be for one of our first postings," she said excitedly.

And then I was off and running, too. "Yes! But first we should write a post introducing our business. I can start working on the blog this weekend."

I was suddenly filled with a fizzy burst of energy. I hadn't touched my blog since getting back from Paris, but it would be fun to start it up again—especially if it could help our business!

Mr. P. chuckled and shook his head. "Together," he said, "you girls sure are an awesome force."

I felt my cheeks flush. "Not without you, Mr. P.," I said. "Without you here helping us, we'd be without a place to work."

Mr. P. smiled and glanced away, as if he was a little embarrassed. "Oh, I'm quite happy to help," he said. "I mean, while I can."

Those last few words stung a little. I wished Mr. P. could stay on and work with us forever. I felt *wishful*. But I knew Ella's dad needed a real job, one that would come with a paycheck. And that meant when a real

job came along, he definitely would have to take it—
and leave us to find another adult chaperone for LPP.
I couldn't imagine anyone who would be more fun and
helpful in the bakery than Mr. P. He wasn't even gone
yet, but already I felt *wistful*.

To get our blog up and running, my first post was
an introduction to our business. I shared a photo of
Bonbon, our mascot, sitting next to our bakery cart.
Along with the photo, I wrote:

*Do you know why Bonbon is the mascot for La Petite
Pâtisserie? Here are five good reasons:*

1. She's adorable!

*2. She's named after the popular French candy—
the bonbon—which is strong (hard) on the outside
and sweet on the inside.*

3. She's a French bulldog.

4. She's from France. When I was learning French baking
   at my aunt and uncle's pâtisserie in Paris, this little stray
   showed up needing food and water—and a home.

5. I flew home with Bonbon AND the idea of starting a French
   baking business with my friends!

My next entry was about what we were baking—
and what we were *botching*. Sometimes mistakes could
be the most fun things to write about!

*When the dishes pile up at the bakery, we use a dishwasher.
But yesterday, when we were all tired, somebody made a
mistake. Instead of using dishwasher detergent, she put in
dish soap. Dish soap makes suds—lots and lots of suds. We all
knew something was wrong when the suds started spilling
out from the dishwasher door and across the floor! Now we
have the cleanest bakery floor in the world. Oh, and the somebody who made the mistake? It's a secret.*

My friends and I fell into a nice rhythm in my

grandparents' kitchen. When we met up at the bakery, we were all business—I mean, pretty much. We always played French music to get us in the mood to bake. Though we talked and laughed as we worked, we had orders to fill and deliver, and we had to stay focused.

Our weekday afternoons were short, so we had to work fast so that we could each get home for dinner and finish our homework. On Saturdays, though, we had more time. We started at noon—or even earlier if we had big orders to fill.

With the help of Mr. P. and his van, deliveries became much easier—especially now that the weather was turning colder.

And Grandma and Grandpa were a huge help, too. They usually lingered for a while after we arrived to answer questions or offer advice. But sometimes, at the end of their own long workdays, they looked so *tired*. I hoped they didn't feel like they had to stick around. I loved it when they helped us, but Mr. P. was there if we needed anything.

One day, when we got to the bakery after school and Grandma looked especially worn out, I asked my friends if we could skip baking. "Grandma and Grandpa will go home early if we're not here," I explained.

"That's okay with me," Ella said.

Maddy nodded in agreement. "We can make a run to the Kitchen Shop to buy more supplies."

"We're almost out of our little boxes," Ella added.

But when my grandparents heard where we were going, Grandma stopped us at the door. "If you're in a pinch or you need something special that you can only get from Mr. Hammond, then going to the Kitchen Shop makes sense," Grandma explained. "But you're paying retail prices there. When you're in business, you need to buy in bulk—or buy lots of supplies at one time—so that you can pay _wholesale_ prices."

"Let me guess," Ella said. "Wholesale is cheaper?"

Grandpa nodded. "Often half the price of what you buy at retail prices."

"That's right," Grandma agreed. "Wholesale means you'll be cutting your costs in half. Let me put it this way: Mr. Hammond buys products at wholesale prices and then charges the retail price."

"Is that against the law?" I asked.

Mr. P. chuckled as he opened his laptop to check for orders. "It's not illegal," he said. "If you're buying a lot of something, companies are willing to sell it to you for less. It's how business is done."

Grandma nodded as she walked over to a metal cabinet and pulled out a thick catalogue. "There's no reason why you can't order from the wholesaler we use," she said, handing me the catalogue.

As I flipped through the pages, I saw that they were filled with packaging of all shapes and sizes. It *was* much cheaper than what we were paying at the Kitchen Shop.

We were learning so much from my grandparents! I only hoped they were getting something out of our being there, too.

One afternoon, while we were looking at other online baking blogs for ideas, I pointed to the screen. "A baking contest? I wonder what that's all about?"

Mr. P. clicked on the contest posting. Up popped information about a regional baking contest.

"It's sponsored by the Massachusetts School of Cooking," Ella said, scanning the screen. "It looks like it's just for kids here in Massachusetts."

I read the details. They were looking for an original recipe by a baker under the age of fifteen. The top winner would receive . . .

"Whoa!" I said, reading aloud now. "One thousand dollars?"

Ella said, "That's huge!"

"Definitely," Maddy said. "We should come up with a recipe! When's the deadline?"

Ella pointed at the screen. "November eleventh," she read. "That's only two weeks away!"

I felt a flood of energy at the thought of experimenting with a new recipe. But we'd have to get started right away. With schoolwork, a Halloween costume to make, orders to fill, and trying to keep our blog up-to-date, I didn't really have a lot of extra time for the contest.

But then Mr. P. tapped the screen. "Uh-oh. Looks like you girls can't enter as LPP," he pointed out. "It says they accept only one submission form: 'One baker, one recipe.'"

Maddy sighed and slumped down into a chair.

Just as quickly as my own enthusiasm had bubbled up, it petered out and my shoulders sagged. I shrugged and turned away to hide my disappointment.

It was time to clean up, so I grabbed the broom and dustpan. As I swept the flour dust into tidy little piles on the linoleum floor, I tried to convince myself that we didn't really have time for the contest anyway. But even though I had plenty of work to do, my mind was thinking about creating an award-winning recipe.

The Great Robot Invasion

Chapter 7

On Friday morning—October 30th—I wrapped the box I'd spray-painted silver in a huge black plastic bag and got a ride to school with Mom. Even though I'd told her about our class's robot project, with hopes that I'd hook her into coming up with fun costumes for her own class, she didn't seem to take the bait.

"Have fun today," she said, as I awkwardly lifted the bagged box from the trunk.

I tried to smile, but I knew that after today, Ella and Maddy would be disappointed once again that they weren't in Mr. Bauer's class, too.

Mr. Bauer taped paper over the window of our classroom door so that no one would pass by and see us putting on our robot costumes. Some of my class-mates had gone all out by adding legs and arms made out of plastic or cardboard tubes.

As I pulled my silver box up over my skirt, Mr. Bauer said, "Hey, Grace, it looks like you're a special kind of robot. Tell us about it."

I pulled one of Grandpa's white baker's hats onto my head and then glanced down at all the things I'd glued or taped onto my robot body: a wooden spoon, a spatula, a set of measuring spoons, two different-size whisks, plus a booklet of recipes I'd printed out and made into a mini cookbook.

"I'm Bistro, the baking robot," I announced. I was actually pretty proud of my costume. I'd taken Josh's advice and really made it my own.

"Clever!" Mr. Bauer's smile was big and wide. Then he turned to the class and said, "Robots come in many forms and with countless functions."

After we each had a chance to say a little something about the robot costumes we'd created, we lined up at the door.

"Bentwick Elementary, here we come!" announced Captain Bauer.

Just as we had rehearsed, we entered the hall and began making robot noises:

"Zip, zip, zip! Zip, zip, zip!"

The Great Robot Invasion

"*Ticka-ticka-ticka-ticka . . . Choo!*"

"*Ping! Ping! Ping!*"

"*Pop, pop, poppa, pop. Pop, pop, poppa, pop.*"

"*Zee-bop. Zee-bop.*"

We walked slowly, pausing by each classroom until the teachers and their students came out to see what we were doing.

Soon the halls echoed with laughing and clapping.

"Go, robots!" somebody called out.

We circled the school, making our way slowly back toward our classroom. But just as we neared my mom's classroom, Mr. Bauer held up his hand.

We robots fell silent.

Suddenly we heard the sounds of gurgling water and birdcalls.

Mr. Bauer pointed to the open door leading to my mom's classroom. Mom was standing at the door with a huge smile on her face. She waved us inside.

As we filed into the classroom, I was stunned. The room had been completely transformed into a tropical garden. Paper murals stretched around the walls, covered with paintings of green trees, plants, and flowers. Near the door, a fountain that I recognized from Mom's summer garden at home spurted water down a series of fake rocks into a pool below. All around the room, real plants sprouted from large containers.

The birdsong we heard matched a group of colorful birds in flight on the computerized whiteboard. And in the middle of the room, Mom's students—all dressed in green shirts, skirts, and pants—sat around a shimmery blue lake on the floor, pretending to fish. Then, at my mom's instruction, they began to whistle like birds. My mom had turned her classroom into something magical in her very own way.

As I rounded the room, Ella and Maddy smiled and waved at me, and I beamed back.

When all of us robots had walked around Mom's classroom, Mr. Bauer raised his arm like a conductor and then started us off down the hall again, making our robot music. I'd never had so much fun at school before!

That day at lunch, I couldn't wait to join Ella and Maddy at their table. "I loved your robot!" Ella said, inching over on the bench to make room.

"A baking robot!" Maddy added. "I should have guessed!"

"And I loved your tropical classroom!" I said. "It was a surprise—just like you thought, Ella."

Maddy beamed. "I had such a blast painting the murals," she said proudly.

"We're keeping it tropical all of next week, too," Ella added with excitement.

In that moment, I was certain of this: Ella and Maddy were having just as much fun in my mom's class as I was in Mr. Bauer's class. Mom was as creative as Mr. Bauer, just in a different way.

On the first Saturday in November, before my grandparents left the bakery, Grandpa waved me out of the kitchen and toward the bakery counter. "Grace? Can you come visit with us for a second?"

I nodded and then called to Mr. P. and my friends, "Be right back." I left them dancing to a French pop song as they filled Mr. P.'s van with boxes for delivery.

Grandma stepped out from behind the counter
to give me a quick hug. She tilted her head at me and
smiled, but there was sad or serious—or both—behind
her eyes. I wondered what could be bothering her.

"We want you and your family to come over tonight
for dinner," Grandma said. "We have something to talk
about."

"Um . . . okay," I said quietly.

Then Grandma glanced away, as if unable to meet
my eyes—as if what she and Grandpa needed to talk
about with us was really serious. My stomach fluttered.
Now I was definitely worried.

Grandpa rested his hand on my shoulder, but instead of feeling warm and comforting, it felt heavy. "It's
about the business," he added. "There's a problem—"

Just then, Mr. P. popped his head through the
swinging door. "The van's loaded up, Grace. We're
ready to go."

I looked back at Grandma and Grandpa. *What was
the problem with the business?*

"Go ahead. Make your deliveries," Grandpa said,
squeezing my shoulder.

"Are you sure?" I asked. I felt torn. I needed to go,

but I wanted to know what was going on with First Street Family Bakery.

"Yes," Grandma said. "We'll talk tonight."

Then, almost as if in slow motion, Grandma turned the sign on the front door to "Closed" and gave me a small wave good-bye. When she and Grandpa stepped outside, a dried leaf fell on Grandpa's head of white hair. He brushed it away wearily and locked the front door. I stood planted, watching them disappear.

There's a problem.

Were my friends and I becoming a burden to my grandparents? Were we going to be kicked out of our baking space?

I forced myself to go back to the kitchen. The others had just finished cleaning up.

"Let's go!" Ella said.

Maddy and I climbed into the middle seat, and Ella sat in front by her dad. As we pulled away from the bakery, Maddy started singing "Frère Jacques." I did my best to join in, even though my throat felt tight.

"Where to first?" Mr. P. asked.

Ella read off the first customer address from the list we'd printed from our website. Yesterday, we'd mapped out the route, and today—smooth as silk—all we had to do was drive to each location and deliver the orders.

I could only hope the "talk" Grandma and Grandpa planned for tonight would go as smoothly. But the twisted knot between my ribs told me otherwise.

When we returned to the bakery, Ella and Mr. P. told us they had an announcement. I braced myself. Had Mr. P. found a new job? I didn't think I could handle that news *and* bad news from Grandma and Grandpa all in one day.

But it wasn't bad news.

"It's payday again," Ella announced with a grin, holding up her business notebook. "Last month, we made more money than we spent!"

"Really?" I said, exhaling with relief. I still couldn't believe we were getting paid to do something that was so much fun. And honestly, I'd been too busy lately to think about making money.

"Cool!" Maddy said.

Ella had a check for Mr. P. to reimburse him for gas, a check for Mom and Dad to start paying back what we owed them, and a check for Grandpa and Grandma. "Grace, will you make sure they get this?"

I looked at the check. "Fifty dollars? I wish we could give them more. They've been so good to us."

Mr. P. swept his arm toward the counters and ovens. "That's for sure. This space is perfect."

"With the way business is going, we should be able to pay them more before long," Ella added.

"Okay," I said, folding the check carefully. As I tucked it into my pocket, I thought about the looks on my grandparents' faces. My business was doing so well. What was happening with their business?

Maddy started to put away her own check, but then paused and asked, "Did you take money out for taxes and supplies?" she asked Ella.

Ella nodded. "Yup. Dad helped me figure out what we needed to save for taxes. After that, I took out a third for supplies, and the other two thirds we can save or spend."

We'd agreed early on that we would reinvest some of our money back into supplies for the business, save some for our dream trip to Paris, and then spend the rest on whatever we wanted. "The three S's, right, Ella?" I said. "Supplies, Save, and Spend."

"Very good, Miss Thomas," Ella said in a teacherly

voice. She was joking, but the truth was, she was really good at this math and money stuff.

"If business keeps going this well, I'll be able to buy my own printer soon!" Maddy exclaimed. She had been using her parents' printer to create all of our labels and pamphlets, but it was an older model. She'd been talking about getting a new one for weeks now.

"I'm going clothes shopping this weekend!" Ella added.

"I might pay to take an online French course," I said quietly, but then I paused. If Grandma and Grandpa were kicking us out of the bakery, we might not be able to do *any* of this. No printer. No clothes shopping. No online French course. No dream trip to Paris. How would I break that to my friends?

"Are you okay, Grace?" Ella asked. "You look like you've got a lot on your mind."

I sighed. "My grandparents invited my family to dinner tonight at their house. It must be important, because . . ." I stopped myself. Until I met with them, I shouldn't assume they were going to ask us to leave their bakery. And if I was right and we *were* being kicked out, I couldn't bear to share that news with my friends just yet. "Well, I'm sure it's fine," I finished.

"Is it their anniversary or something?" Maddy asked.

I hesitated. It was definitely something, but what? "No, their anniversary is in June. I think they just want to get together," I said, with forced cheerfulness. A lump rose in my throat and I swallowed hard.

All through dinner, I kept a careful eye on Grandpa and Grandma, wondering when they were going to share their news. Grandpa ate every bite of the pork chops baked with apricots. Grandma finished her slice of rhubarb pie. But I could barely eat.

"For someone who doesn't like to bake," Grandma said to Mom, "this pie is just delicious."

"Well, it helps that I like to garden," said Mom. "I had so much rhubarb last summer that I had to freeze it. Can't let it go to waste, y'know."

Grandma's smile softened, and she said half-seriously, "Does that mean you're ready to take over First Street Family Bakery?"

Mom laughed. "That would be the day!"

Grandma winked. "I know, dear. I'm just teasing. Say, are you running a half marathon again anytime soon?"

Mom buttered a slice of sourdough bread. "Once school started, I decided it's just too much to try to do it all. I'll start training again next spring and do the Last Blast of Summer run again."

Conversation ambled like a shallow stream over rocks. Dad talked about snow coming soon and being ready for it by giving his skis a good base coating of wax. Josh talked about putting fat tires on a bike so he could bike through the winter, snow or not. And I tried to force down my whipped yams and green beans with slivered almonds, and waited for the real reason we had gotten together tonight.

After dinner, we went into the TV room. I was surprised to see that Grandpa had set up his old slide projector and screen.

"That thing's an antique!" Josh said.

"Sometimes old things work best," Grandpa replied. "I'm proof of that," he added with a chuckle.

Grandma patted the empty space on the couch

beside her. "Come sit with me, Grace."

I didn't hesitate. I scooted in close to Grandma and pressed myself against her side.

Anxiety swelled in my chest.

Whatever is wrong with the business, I wanted to tell her, *let me be able to help.*

But I said nothing. I just waited and worried.

Once we were all settled, Grandpa dimmed the lights and started clicking slides from the past. There were slides of Mom when she was little—an adorable one of her holding a white rabbit—and slides of her and Aunt Sophie. And there were slides of the bakery, from the very beginning.

In many slides, Aunt Sophie was working in the bakery's kitchen, wearing various aprons. I recognized the one decorated with apples. I still wore that apron sometimes when I worked in the bakery!

Looking at the slides, I almost felt as if that little girl in the apron were me. Aunt Sophie and I had both grown up loving baking. Now Aunt Sophie was a baker and living her dream in Paris. Who knew where my love of baking would take me next?

Anxiety swelled again in my chest. But as Grandma

laughed aloud at some of the photos and Grandpa told short bits of stories about funny customers, I began to relax. Maybe they'd simply wanted to get together with us to do *this*—to celebrate all the good times we'd had at the bakery and as a family.

The slide show ended with an image of the bakery, with its faded lettering above the front door. It must have been taken recently, because the nearby maple tree was a brilliant red and I recognized a recent LPP flyer posted in the bakery window.

"And here's where our journey comes to an end," Grandpa said. "With great sadness, yet with wonderful memories, Grandma and I have come to a painful decision."

I sucked in my breath. Here was the news—finally. I dreaded what was coming next.

"Grandpa, did I do something wrong?" I blurted. "My friends and I try to leave the bakery kitchen sparkling clean and to always turn the lights out when we go and to follow—"

"No, darling. It's not about you girls or anything you did," Grandma said quickly, patting my leg. "Don't think that for a second."

"It's about First Street Family Bakery," Grandpa said, his voice catching a little. "We've decided to put it up for sale."

Up for sale? The bakery? I couldn't believe what I'd just heard. If my grandparents were going to shut down their business, then my business would have to close, too.

Everyone was silent. The only sound in the room was the *whir* of the projector fan.

For Sale

Chapter 8

$\mathcal{T}$ he full force of Grandpa's words hit me. "You're selling the bakery?" I said. "But . . . you've had it for as long as I can remember. And . . . you love it, and . . . we *need* it for *La Petite Pâtisserie*!"

Tears welled up in my eyes, partly because I'd been holding back all of my anxiety about hearing the bad news, and partly because now the bad news was terrible in a totally unexpected way.

Grandma pulled me close. "All of that is true, honey, but we've had to borrow money the past few years to stay in business. When you girls asked if you could use the bakery kitchen, I thought about telling you then—maybe we should have. But we hadn't made up our minds yet. Now, after another month of poor sales, we know we have to sell. I'm so sorry, Grace."

Mom pressed a hand to her cheek. "First Street

For Sale

Family Bakery is going to close? Really? I can't quite believe it."

Mom looked as shocked as I felt.

Grandpa was still standing beside the projector. He shook his head. "Business has died off, plain and simple."

"But what happened?" Dad asked. "Any idea why?"

"City-Way and their new supermarket bakery, for one," Grandpa said with a sigh. "We just can't compete with their discounted prices, and we can't afford to offer the same promotions they do."

"And the drop in business," Grandma added, "means that we just can't keep our doors open much longer."

Josh piped up with forced cheerfulness. "So you're retiring? That's a good thing, right?"

Grandpa shrugged. "Yes and no. It's good when you're ready for it and want to stop working, but not so much when you feel you have no other choice."

Mom got up and hugged Grandma, and then she went to stand by Grandpa. "I'm so sorry, Dad," she said sadly.

I shook my head, trying to take in all this hard

news. "Wait a minute. If you two can't keep the bakery in business, how's anyone else going to?"

"I suppose someone will find another use for the space," Grandma said softly.

"This is just too sad," I whispered. I closed my eyes and felt the warmth of Grandma's hand on my back.

"When will you put it up for sale?" Dad asked, breaking the silence.

I braced myself for the answer.

"Immediately," Grandpa said. "It may take some time for the building to sell. But we're hoping a buyer comes along by the end of the year. We'd like to maybe do some traveling this winter."

"Someplace warm," Grandma added.

"Hey," Josh said. "That doesn't sound so bad. You could take bikes and go exploring."

But I couldn't think about exploring. "The end of the year?" I asked, my voice cracking. "That's so soon!"

And then, with the tiniest hope that it could make a difference, I remembered the money I was supposed to give my grandparents. "Wait a second!" I pulled the check from my jeans pocket and handed it to Grandma. "We want to pay rent. This is fifty dollars."

For Sale

Grandma unfolded the check, and I saw tears glisten in her eyes. "Oh, Grace, darling," she said, "We can't take this from you girls."

I stood up. "No, we want you to, Grandma—you *need* to. Please?"

She set the check on the coffee table. "That's very sweet of you." Then she leveled her gaze on me. "We dreaded telling you, Grace. You and your friends have done an amazing job with *La Petite Pâtisserie*. We hate knowing that our decision to close the bakery and sell the building affects your business."

I didn't want Grandma and Grandpa to feel any worse about what they were doing, but it was one more blow to LPP. "First we had to move out of the kitchen at home," I said quietly. "Now we're all settled into the bakery and things are going really well, and we have to move *again*. But to where?"

Tears ran hot down my face. I felt bad for Grandma and Grandpa that they had to close and sell their bakery after all these years. I couldn't imagine Bentwick or my world without it. But I also felt bad for *me*—I couldn't help it.

Ever since I'd told Grandma and Grandpa about my

dream of starting a business, I'd been working so hard to make it a success. But if First Street Family Bakery couldn't make it, how could *La Petite Pâtisserie*?

All day on Sunday I stewed over Grandma and Grandpa's news, avoiding texts from my friends and hiding out in my bedroom with Bonbon. I didn't even feel like talking with Sylvie. I couldn't bear to tell her that First Street Family Bakery was closing.

I didn't have it in me to break the bad news to Ella and Maddy, either. So I asked my grandparents to do it. On Monday afternoon, as we stepped through the back door of the bakery, Grandma and Grandpa were there to greet us. As we bustled about—washing our hands, putting on aprons, and turning to our whiteboard— Grandma and Grandpa made small talk with Mr. P.

Mr. P. was in an especially good mood. "Hey, girls," he blurted out. "I thought you should know. I'm one of the final two applicants for a job. I should hear by Friday, and if I get it, we'll have to discuss what you girls will do here without me. I could still help out on

❦ For Sale ❧

Saturdays, at least until you find someone else."

What *was* this? Rain-on-my-parade week?

I met Grandma's eyes and bit down on my lip. She could tell I was struggling, so she left Grandpa's side and walked over to me. Then she reached for my hand, gave it a squeeze, and held on. I was grateful, because I was using every ounce of my strength to keep from crying.

Ella wore a mixed expression of happiness for her dad and disappointment for us. She glanced my way and shrugged.

Brace yourself, I wanted to say. *There's worse to come.*

And then Grandpa explained that they were selling the bakery. "I put the 'For Sale' sign in the window this morning."

"What?" Maddy exclaimed. "You can't sell!" But then she caught herself and said a little more calmly, "I mean, of course you can. It's your bakery. But . . . we've worked so hard and . . ." She looked at me and said weakly, "What are we going to do?"

Mr. P. cleared his throat. "I'm sorry to hear your news," he said to my grandparents.

"Oh, maybe it's a blessing in disguise," Grandma

said a little too brightly. "We might get a chance to try life without constantly working—maybe take a vacation or two. Not that we're quite ready to retire, but sometimes you have to accept what life deals out."

"Everything just feels so unfair right now," I said quietly.

"Life isn't fair, Grace," Grandpa said gently. "Never is. Never was. The only thing that evens out the playing field—and the only thing we can control—is our attitude when things get tough."

Maybe Grandpa was right, but I didn't want to hear it right now. No words or advice could set things right.

"You girls can keep using the kitchen until the building sells," Grandma said. "But soon we'll put out our 'Closed' sign for good." Her eyes threatened tears, but she forced a smile.

Grandma and Grandpa left for home. They'd put in a full day of work, but our baking was just beginning.

I turned on some French music, hoping it would help lift our spirits. Instead, we were all very quiet as we worked.

As the last batch of *madeleines* was cooling, Ella sighed. "Maybe it's time for us to just close up, too," she whispered. She glanced back at the sink, where her dad was washing a stack of dishes. "I have a feeling my dad is going to get the job he was telling us about."

Maddy nodded slowly. "We've had fun," she said. "Way more than I ever expected to have. But now, without a space to bake in or an adult to help us . . ."

I stared at my friends in shock. They were ready to call it quits? The last thing in the world I wanted to do was to close the doors on *La Petite Pâtisserie*!

My eyes went to the shelving filled with all of our packaging supplies: sheets of pink tissue paper and cellophane wrap, different-size boxes, and frosty plastic bags stickered with our name and logo. I'd poured my heart into this business. *We'd* poured ourselves into it. How could everyone act like it was time to close up and move on?

Mr. P. was done at the sink. I said, "Maybe you guys should just go home." I tried to keep my voice steady. "I want to finish up here on my own today."

Mr. P. studied my face and then nodded. "Fair enough. Let's go, girls, and give Grace a little time alone."

As Ella and Maddy gathered their things and left

the kitchen, Ella tried to catch my eye. But I couldn't look at her. I was angry and sad and afraid I would cry. I turned my back until I heard the door to the alley close softly.

Then I stepped through the swinging doors into the front of the bakery. I took it all in, trying to memorize every detail of the display cases and cash register. But as I looked around, I realized something. Though my memories were filled with bright laughter and wonderful smells, I now saw the bakery in a different light.

The shop looked faded and dull. It looked exactly the way I was feeling.

Tired.

Discouraged.

Worn out.

I took another look at the "Closed" sign on the door of the bakery. It couldn't really be closed forever, could it?

Then I traced my finger along the top of the "For Sale" sign in the front window. I wanted to take it down and chuck it out onto the street.

Closed *could* be forever. And I'd probably better start getting used to the idea.

For Sale

As I stepped back into the kitchen, I reached up and started yanking images of Paris from the walls—one after another. Who needs inspiration when a dream comes to an end?

I gathered the images into a small stack and then walked over to the recycling bin, ready to toss them in. But I couldn't do it—I couldn't even open my hand.

Tears started to fall, and a drop fell on a picture of a pigeon atop a fountain in Paris. With my free hand, I swiped at my eyes.

I just couldn't let go of what I loved. At least not yet.

Instead, I walked to the metal cabinet and opened it. I pulled out the thick wholesale catalogue, flipped to the middle, and placed the stack of French images inside carefully so that they wouldn't curl. I closed the catalogue and returned it to the cabinet. Then I left, locking the door behind me.

The day was warm for early November, and I was grateful to bike home alone with just my thoughts. But like my bike tires, my thoughts just went around and around in circles. We were on the verge of losing Mr. P., and soon we'd lose the bakery kitchen, too. Ella and Maddy probably were right that we should just close LPP and move on. But how could I?

I needed some serious cheering up, and I knew the perfect dog who could help me.

I found Bonbon in the backyard playing with Zulu. Josh was sitting on the steps doing his homework.

"Hey," I said, sitting down beside him.

"Hey," he replied.

Bonbon dashed up to me, licked me on the cheek, and darted off again to chase Zulu.

"Thanks for bringing Zulu over for a playdate," I said to my brother.

"Sure," Josh replied. "Figured I'd better keep an eye on them so I wouldn't get in trouble with Mom . . ."

"Yeah, she wouldn't be happy if they dug up the hundred bulbs she just planted for next spring."

Next spring. By then, LPP would be just an old memory. My eyes started to burn again, so I tried to think about something else.

Luckily, that's when Mom called to us from the back door. "Come on inside, you two. Dinner's ready."

At the table, I did my best to focus on eating. Mom had made my favorite: spaghetti and meatballs, Caesar salad, and garlic bread with lots of butter. But halfway through dinner, I was just twirling my noodles around and around. I didn't have an appetite.

"Grace," Dad said, "if you're not going to eat, please talk. Tell us what's on your mind. It's not good to bottle up your emotions."

I spun my fork a few more rotations, dragging the spaghetti with it.

"What's up?" Josh asked. "You've only eaten one meatball and almost no noodles. You usually devour a plate of spaghetti in five minutes."

I stopped, set my fork on my plate, and dropped my hands to the sides of my chair. Bonbon, who spent dinnertime under the table, pushed her wet nose into my palm. Sweet girl—she seemed to understand why I was upset without me saying a word.

"Mr. P. is probably getting a job," I said slowly, trying to make my parents understand how bad things had gotten. "He'll find out Friday."

"I didn't know Mr. Petronia had a job opportunity," Dad said. "Now you'll need to find another adult to supervise your baking."

"Why bother?" I said bleakly. "Pretty soon we won't have any place to bake."

Mom sighed. "I feel sad that the bakery is closing, too," she said. "I realize Grandma and Grandpa can't run it forever, but it's still hard for me to think of it not being there."

Dad nodded. "This is a big change for both of you."

"I really, *really* don't want to close LPP," I said, fighting back tears. "I don't want to stop filling orders. I don't want to stop baking." I took a deep breath. "Everything feels like it's falling apart. I just want someone to fix it."

"Grace, honey," Dad said. "This is a hard place to be right now. But sometimes we need to learn to accept what is."

"You should be proud of what you've done, Grace," Mom said gently. "You and your friends gave it your best shot and had lots of fun doing it."

Mom was already talking about my business as if it were gone. I couldn't listen to another word. I stood and raced upstairs to my bedroom, Bonbon following close behind. I closed my door and flopped down on my bed.

I wished I could talk with Sylvie, Aunt Sophie, and Uncle Bernard. They'd understand how important my

business was to me. But it was too late to go online
with them now. It was after midnight in Paris. All
I could do was wrap my arms around Bonbon and cry
myself to sleep.

Dreams of Paris
Chapter 9

*L*ike one of the painted turtles I often spotted in the canal, I paddled slowly through Tuesday. I tried to focus on what Mr. Bauer was saying, but my head was tucked inside my shell and my mind was scrambling around the same questions I'd asked myself all night.

Why did Grandma and Grandpa have to sell their bakery? Where could LPP find another kitchen to use? What if Mr. P. got the job? Who could fill in for him so that we could continue our business? Could we continue on at all, or was I being wistful, hanging on when clearly nothing was going my way?

Maybe Dad was right. Maybe I had to learn to accept what is.

Tap, tap, tap.

It was Marcos, tapping the back of my head again.

I spun around to see him holding up the eraser end of his pencil.

"I wasn't sleeping," I said.

"Well, you must have been somewhere else," he said. "Didn't you hear the bell?"

I glanced around the room. Everyone was packing up their backpacks and clearing off their desks. School was over? I wasn't just paddling through my day like a turtle; I'd flopped all the way over onto my back and needed help righting myself.

"No," I admitted. "I was concentrating on something else."

"What kid doesn't hear the bell at the end of the day?" he asked with a grin.

"Me, apparently," I answered, gathering my things. "I just have a lot on my mind."

Marcos stood and flung his black-and-yellow backpack over his shoulder. "I guess that happens when you run your own business."

Not for long, I wanted to say. Instead, I just shrugged.

He tilted his head and said, "Not many kids our age could do what you're doing. I think it's cool."

Sometimes, just the tiniest speck of encouragement

can go a long way. What Marcos said made me feel better—a little more hopeful, somehow.

"Thanks." I smiled at Marcos.

After I waved good-bye to Mr. Bauer, I walked down the hall to Mom's room. I was supposed to ride home with her, but she wasn't quite ready to leave. While I waited for her to finish up at her desk, I wandered over to her room's reading corner and sank down in a purple stuffed chair.

Mom's classroom was still decorated like a tropical garden. As my eyes traced the painted plants and flowers on the mural, my ears soaked up the sound of water trickling down the nearby fountain. I didn't feel like I was sitting in school in Bentwick, Massachusetts. I'd been transported halfway across the world.

For a moment, I wished I were a student in *this* classroom. It looked completely different from the way it had before Halloween, when it was just a regular fourth-grade classroom. Mom had transformed it.

It's too bad Mom can't transform Grandma and Grandpa's business, I thought. *If only a mural and a fountain could turn it back into a busy bakery again.*

Dreams of Paris

When Mom and I arrived home, Bonbon seemed to know I'd had a hard day. As I leaned down to say hello, she stood up on her little back legs and kissed my chin.

"Oh, Bonbon," I said. "I needed that."

Then I took her outside, breathing in the earthy autumn-scented air. Some leaves clung to the treetops, but more had fallen to the ground. After the next brisk wind, the branches would be bare.

A strong sense of longing filled me. I thought of all the hours Maddy and Ella and I had spent together, working so hard to turn our ideas into reality. I even missed our disasters, like the time a bag of flour exploded across the floor and a wet dog tromped through it and all through the house. *Were we really going to have to give it all up?*

Bonbon now had her nose buried deep in leaves, snorting and snuffling, as if she might come face-to-face with a squirrel. She made me laugh out loud.

"Bonbon, you have the right idea," I said to her. I dropped to my knees, and soon we were playing hide-and-go-seek in the leaves.

As we played, my heaviness began to lift. "You're good for me, you know that?" I said to her. In response, she dropped her head to her paws, her little rump up in the air, and wagged her tail.

"Better run!" I teased. I took three steps toward her. "I'm gonna getcha!"

With that, she darted off around the yard in circles, coming almost close enough for me to catch her before she dashed off again.

When we finally went inside, Mom turned from chopping carrots and onions. "Your cheeks are rosy," she said. "It looked like you two were having fun together."

I nodded. "We were."

"It's good to see your smile again," Mom said, adding the chopped veggies to a steaming pot of chicken broth. "It's good to take a break and do something that makes you happy."

I sat down on the floor with Bonbon and brushed her coat. She especially loves being brushed under her chin. And eventually, she rolled onto her back so that I could brush her belly, too, where her skin spots show through. She has black-and-white fur on the outside, but her skin is black and white, too.

I thought about Mom's advice. Next to time with Bonbon, there was one thing that always made me happy: baking. Maybe I could bake a Bonbon-inspired treat, something black-and-white. But what?

For ideas, I turned to a French cookbook with lots of photos. I looked at a pastry called *gland* filled with a sweet custard and decorated with black-and-white frosting. And then there was the *religieuse*, a fancy layered dessert with vanilla and chocolate icing.

I decided to experiment. I'd make something of my own, drawing from these other recipes. My mind started "stirring" together possibilities: chocolate batter and vanilla batter blended with a little French *je ne sais quoi*—I don't know what—to come up with something tasty, artsy, and amazing. Now I couldn't wait to get started!

"Mom? Mind if I bake something?" I asked.

She smiled—as if my wanting to bake was another good sign that I was going to be okay. "You go right ahead."

Before I knew it, I was humming along, stirring up two different batters. It felt good to bake just for the fun of it. There were plenty of orders to fill for LPP, but those would have to wait. For now, I was going to enjoy some "Grace time" in the kitchen.

Every time Mom checked on her chicken-noodle soup and gave it a stir, she glanced over at me. "Are you having fun?" she finally asked.

I met her eyes and nodded.

"That's my girl," she said and smiled back.

That night, after a dinner of soup, grilled cheese sandwiches, and salads, I served up my black-and-white cream-filled creations on dessert plates. But before I did, I took a photo.

Click!

"I want to show Sylvie," I explained. Then I passed plates around the table.

"Whoa!" Josh said after his first bite. "This is good!"

"Agreed," Dad said. "What do you call it?"

"I don't know yet," I said with a grin. But I loved that *they* loved it.

"You made this without a recipe?" Mom asked, lifting another forkful to her mouth. "You whipped this together—just today?"

I nodded. "Yes, Mom. You *saw* me."

She laughed. "I can't imagine not following a recipe. Grace, you definitely take after your grandparents and your aunt—not me. An original recipe? This belongs in a cookbook somewhere!"

An original recipe? Suddenly, the baking contest I'd learned about online popped into my mind. Wasn't the deadline tomorrow? I'd assumed I didn't have time to create a new recipe, but here I'd done just that, without even thinking about the contest. Now, with my family's high praise, I decided, why not enter? I probably wouldn't win, but it would be fun to try!

After dishes, while everything was fresh in my mind, I wrote down the ingredients for my new recipe and some step-by-step directions. But what was I going to call it? Something that reminded me of the first time I'd met Bonbon. Something that sounded French.

Then it came to me. With Mom's help, I went online, found the contest, and entered my recipe. I uploaded the photo that I'd taken. And then I entered the name for my inspiring new dessert:

Dreams of Paris.

After I pressed Send, I felt happier than I had in days. I knew that Grandma and Grandpa's bakery would still be closing. And I knew that *La Petite Pâtisserie* might very well be closing, too. But I could still bake. That wasn't going to change. I suddenly wanted to fill every last order our customers had placed with LPP—and do it with an extra-special touch. But I needed help.

I sent off a quick text to Maddy and Ella: "Meet me at the bakery tomorrow after school. We still have work to do!"

That night, I slept like a rock.

On Saturday morning, I woke up eager to get back to Grandma and Grandpa's kitchen. My friends and I had worked hard on Wednesday and then again last night after school to fill all our orders. Today we would finish up. Was it the last time we'd be baking for LPP?

I also woke up wanting to talk with Sylvie—to finally let her know the news about Grandpa and Grandma's bakery. I calculated the time difference in Paris. "Mom, could we go online for a video-chat with Sylvie? I don't think I can wait until tomorrow."

"We can try," she said. "Let's hope she and Aunt Sophie are around."

Mom and I settled in front of our computer. To my surprise, we didn't catch our French family in their apartment in Paris. Instead, Aunt Sophie answered on her phone. The screen was small.

"*Bonjour!* Hello there!" Aunt Sophie said. "What a pleasant surprise to see you both! You caught us having a late lunch. Look where we are!"

Then she moved her phone around to bring Sylvie and Lily into view. They were sitting outside at a café under a bright sun, wearing jackets and scarves, with sandwiches and bowls of soup on the table in front of them. Lily was bundled from head to toe in pink, and her eyes were bright as she stared at the phone.

"Hello, Grace!" Sylvie's face appeared in front of the screen for a moment.

"*Bonjour,* Sylvie!" I replied.

Mom said, "You must be at the café across the street from the *pâtisserie*, yes?"

Aunt Sophie nodded. "Is everything all right, sis?" she asked. "You don't usually call us out of the blue like this."

Mom didn't let her worry for long. She quickly filled her in on the big news—that Grandma and Grandpa had put their bakery up for sale.

"Oh no," Aunt Sophie said, concern spreading across her face. "That breaks my heart! I thought they still loved running their business."

"They do," Mom said, "but business just isn't what it used to be. They're not keeping up with expenses and can't compete with the low prices of the new super-market bakery in town."

Mom put her arm around me. "And it's not just Mom and Dad's business," she said with a sad sigh. "Grace and her friends may not have a kitchen to use for LPP once First Street Family Bakery closes."

Aunt Sophie shook her head. "I wish there were something I could do," she said after she'd translated the news to Sylvie.

I looked away from the sadness in her eyes. In the background behind her, a woman walked by with a *baguette* under her arm. I could hear a street musician playing an accordion from somewhere nearby. I suddenly missed everything about Paris and wished I was there.

Dreams of Paris

"They say they're not ready to retire," Mom continued, "but maybe it's for the best. Times change. Speaking of change, Sophie, how are you and Bernard managing the bakery now that baby Lily is taking up so much of your time?"

"Oh, very well," Aunt Sophie said, perking back up. "Life is busier, but it's never been better. And business is good. Wait—I'll show you."

Aunt Sophie turned the screen of her phone slowly so that it scanned the neighborhood and rested on her bakery—*La Pâtisserie*. The windows were filled with beautifully displayed treats. A steady stream of customers came and went through the front door, and several more sat outside at inviting little round tables and chairs, enjoying their baked goods.

Everything about *La Pâtisserie*—from the bakery's sign with its scrolled letters to the pink trim around the front windows—brought back a flood of memories from last summer. I had so loved the idea of saving up enough money to return to Paris with my friends. I wanted them to see for themselves what had inspired me to start our French baking business. But now that trip seemed like a distant dream that was out of reach.

In that moment, as I stared at the French *pâtisserie* that I remembered so well, an idea came to me. An idea that I suddenly knew was *magnifique*!

"Sylvie!" I blurted at the screen.

"Oui?" She leaned in closer, alarm in her brown eyes.

"Mom! Aunt Sophie!" I continued.

Mom whirled around to face me, as if I needed emergency care.

My words tumbled out. "What if we gave Grandma and Grandpa's bakery a whole new look? The other day, when I looked at it—*really* looked at it—I realized that it looked old. Dull and faded. It looks nothing like your *pâtisserie,* Aunt Sophie. What if we could help make First Street Family Bakery look more fun, more inviting? Maybe it would help business and Grandma and Grandpa wouldn't have to close."

"Interesting idea," said Aunt Sophie slowly. "What did you have in mind?"

I paused. My great idea didn't have any details—yet. "I'm not sure, exactly," I said. "But for starters, I'm thinking new paint in brighter colors and a new sign. Maybe a few little tables and chairs, inside and outside—like at your *pâtisserie*—so that people would want to sit and stay longer."

Mom pursed her lips. Her eyes told me she didn't want me to get my hopes up. "Remember what your dad said, Grace, about accepting what is?"

"Mom, I can't," I protested. "Not yet, anyway." How could I help her see things my way? Then it came to me. "It's like with your classroom at school, Mom. A new look can change *everything*!"

At that, Mom's eyes softened. The edges of her mouth turned upward, just slightly. "I suppose it doesn't hurt to at least bring up your ideas with your grandparents. See what they have to say."

I beamed.

"And if nothing else," she continued, "a fresh look might help their business sell more quickly."

Sell. That was a word I didn't want to hear!

Aunt Sophie paused to translate the conversation for Sylvie. When she finished, Sylvie's big eyes lit up. "Grace," she said, beaming. *"Je serai ta consultante."*

Aunt Sophie translated, and my eyes lit up, too. "I would love for you to be the consultant!" I said. "Could you start by sending me photos of your *pâtisserie*?"

And with that, Sylvie started to pipe up—in French, of course—with what I assumed were all sorts of great ideas.

"Sylvie said she'll take photos of our *pâtisserie* and of others in the neighborhood to give you some ideas," Aunt Sophie explained. "She can send them to you by tomorrow morning."

I met Sylvie's smile.

"*Merci beaucoup*, Sylvie!"

By the end of our video-chat, I felt the familiar fizzy energy surge through me. I didn't have the answers for everything, but it sure felt good to have a plan.

A Painting Party
Chapter 10

$\mathcal{B}$ y the following morning, my e-mail in-box
was full of photos that Sylvie had taken of her
family's *pâtisserie* and other bakeries in her St. Germain
neighborhood. I printed the photos out and sat
down to look at them, but something—or a couple of
some*ones*—was missing. I needed my friends!

Ella and Maddy came over as soon as they could,
and that's when my best idea struck. "Mom, do you
think we could video-chat with Sylvie right now?"

I was sure that Sylvie could help us figure out some
new colors and decorations for my grandparents'
bakery. Plus, it would be cool for her to finally "meet"
my friends.

With Ella on my right and Maddy on my left, we
squeezed (just barely) onto the computer chair and
waited to connect with Sylvie's computer in Paris.

Bleep! With a small wave, and her thick sandy hair in a side-pony, Sylvie appeared on the screen. "Hello, Grace!"

"*Bonjour*, Sylvie!" My heart warmed at seeing her. Though we were an ocean apart, it felt almost like we were sisters. "Sylvie, this is my friend Ella."

Ella waved at the screen. "*Bonjour*, Sylvie. I have heard lots about you!"

"And this is Maddy," I said next, wrapping my arm around my red-haired friend.

Maddy giggled and blew Sylvie a kiss. "Hello!" she said.

Sylvie smiled shyly. "Hello, Ella and Maddy. It is nice to meet you."

Aunt Sophie popped in for a moment, next to Sylvie. "I'm here, girls, if you need any translating, okay?"

With a little French and a little English—and a little help from Aunt Sophie—the four of us managed to have a conversation about how to help save my grand-parents' bakery.

With the photos printed out on the table around us, Maddy said, "Sylvie, I love the photos you sent of the *pâtisseries.* They're so colorful! I wish I could step inside every one of them."

"Sylvie," I asked, "what colors do you think we should use if we repaint Grandma and Grandpa's bakery?"

Aunt Sophie was there to translate for us.

Sylvie rested her mouth on her fist with a "hmm." Then her eyes lit up. *"Rouge,"* she said, pronouncing her "r" the way the French do. *"Rose,"* she added thoughtfully. And then, with a smile, she suggested one more color, as if it were the finishing touch on a cake. *"Et bleu clair!"*

Aunt Sophie smiled. "That would be red, pink, and light blue."

"Ooh . . . I like those colors!" said Maddy. She tried to repeat the colors in French, and pretty soon we were all saying them together.

"Rouge, rose, et bleu clair!" we practiced in unison for Sylvie.

In return, she tried them in English for us. She could say "red, pink, and light blue" pretty well in English, but her accent was still wonderfully French.

By the time we hung up with Sylvie, I was flying

high. It felt great to brainstorm with my friends some creative ways to help First Street Family Bakery stay open!

Armed with the images Sylvie had sent of French *pâtisseries*, and encouraged by Ella's and Maddy's enthusiasm, Mom and I invited Grandma and Grandpa over to our house for a family bonfire that night.

In the backyard fire pit, the flames flickered red and yellow, shooting tiny sparks skyward. We sat in a circle of lawn chairs around the fire, roasting marshmallows for s'mores over the low blue flames.

"Whatcha cooking up now, Grace, besides that marshmallow?" Grandpa asked. "I can tell that your wheels are turning."

I was barely able to contain my enthusiasm. "Sylvie and my friends and I have some ideas on how to rescue the bakery!"

"Oh?" Grandpa said, fixing his gaze on the marshmallow on the end of his stick. He was turning the stick over and over and didn't look up.

A Painting Party

I pressed ahead. "We think that if you could give it a new look, make it stand out in a whole new way, you might not have to sell it."

Grandma sighed. "At this point, Grace," she said, "we don't have extra money for major remodeling. We'll leave that to the building's next owners."

"But our plan shouldn't cost a lot," I said, sitting up straight in my chair. "We just need some paint, which my friends and I want to help pay for. We also need tables and chairs, and there are plenty of those at Maddy's parents' antique shop. They said they'd give you a great deal." I was talking fast, my excitement building. "And maybe window boxes," I added. "Those are Mom's specialty. I've got pictures of my ideas inside," I said, standing up. "Come on! I'll show you!"

Grandpa grunted a little, which I took as a good sign. "Well, let me finish my s'more, at least," he said, pressing the gooey marshmallow between two graham crackers.

I tried not to tap my toe impatiently while I waited for Grandpa to eat. When he finally finished, we all went inside. I spread out Sylvie's images on our dining room table. The photos showed the cheerful interiors and bright exteriors of a bunch of bakeries in Paris.

Grandma tapped an image of *La Pâtisserie*. "Why, that's Sophie and Bernard's bakery, isn't it?"

I nodded. "Sylvie took these photos," I said. Then I explained that we'd video-chatted to discuss how to help the bakery. "If we give it a new look, maybe we'll bring in more customers. Besides," I added, "you'd help *La Petite Pâtisserie* by staying open, too."

"I don't know," Grandpa said, with a wag of his head. "All this pink and red—well, it's just not me."

I'd been expecting that. "I know, Grandpa," I said quickly. "But what you *love* is baking, and if this plan works to bring in more customers, then you could *keep* doing what you love."

Josh joined in. "Yeah, Grandpa, you'd be back in the kitchen and you wouldn't have to even look at the remodeled part while you're baking."

I shot Josh a grateful look.

"I'm too old for these changes," Grandpa said, more firmly this time. "Thanks for trying, Grace, really. But we've made up our minds."

Grandma studied the photos. She didn't say a word, but the corners of her lips turned up ever so slightly.

A Painting Party

A train whistled in the distance.

"Grandpa," I said, the whistle reminding me of all of his talks about history and change. "Remember what you said about the railroad? You talked about the American Industrial Revolution. You said that when trains came along, they stopped using barges on the canals because the trains were so much faster."

"Yeah, that's what I said," Grandpa said warily.

"Well, doesn't that show that change can be *good*?"

Grandpa looked at Grandma, and then he met my eyes. "You sure are full of big ideas, Grace."

Grandma put her hand over Grandpa's. "I see no harm in trying. Do you?" she asked. "Grace and her friends have put a lot of thought into this."

Grandpa hesitated, and then raised his hands in the air as if surrendering. "What can I say?" he said. "I guess if nothing else, giving the bakery a fresh look might help it sell faster."

Those words again. That was *not* what I wanted to hear! But at least we had Grandma and Grandpa's go-ahead to try out our plan, and all I could do now was hope that it *worked*.

When you have a good idea, there's no sense in putting it off. Right after Grandma and Grandpa went home, I sent out a group e-mail:

You're invited!!!
Who? You and your family!
Where? First Street Family Bakery
When? 8:00 a.m. – 5:00 p.m., this Saturday and Sunday
Why? To give it a face-lift!
Why #2? To keep it in business!
What? We'll brainstorm and paint!

The message went off to Maddy's parents, Ella's parents, Grandma and Grandpa, Mom and Dad, and Josh. Grandma and Grandpa had agreed to close the bakery for the weekend. Two days didn't give us very much time. I hoped we could get everything done!

Mom, to my surprise, seemed just as excited about our plan as I was. She went online for the latest weather updates every day that week.

"Unseasonably warm for the next few days," she

reported on Wednesday, "with possible snow showers early next week. Guess we'd better 'seize the day'!"

We cornered Dad into helping us build wooden flower boxes for the storefront.

"Isn't it too late for flowers?" Dad asked, raising an eyebrow.

"Yes, but we can fill them with pine cones and cedar boughs," I answered.

"And if we plant hyacinth and tulip bulbs now," Mom said, "they'll come up next spring."

I smiled at Mom's words. She must have thought it was possible that Grandma and Grandpa could still be in business next spring.

Before the week was over, Mom drove my friends and me to the local hardware store. We studied a zillion color samples, trying to find some that matched the color scheme we had chosen. We finally settled on "Cherry Red" for the exterior, "Powder Blue" for the interior, and "Pink Icing" for the trim throughout.

The store clerk mixed up several gallons of paint and locked them one at a time in a cabinet to shake them up. As the paint cans vibrated, I hugged Ella and Maddy. "I'm excited. We picked great colors!"

"*Oui, oui,*" Maddy chimed in.

At the dinner table Friday night, I looked at Mom, Dad, and Josh. "Thanks, guys," I said.

"For what?" Josh replied.

"For supporting my wild ideas," I said with a grin.

Dad put his arm around my shoulder. "They are wildly creative ideas," he said. "But then, we're a wildly creative family, yes?"

"Yes!" I said. "I've been thinking about that. Dad, honestly, if you ever wanted to start a business making birdhouses . . . Or Mom, if you ever wanted to sell more of your garden ornaments . . ."

Mom cracked up and made a time-out sign with her hands. "Let's just focus on one small business at a time, okay?"

I agreed, but I could tell that I'd made my parents feel good. We *were* a creative family—from my baker grandparents to my brother, who could make up melodies on the piano. I knew that *together,* we could make a difference at the bakery. We could help First Street Family Bakery *and* LPP!

A Painting Party

By eight o'clock on Saturday morning, a big crew
had shown up at the bakery.

Mr. P. brought a ladder and drop cloths to protect
the floors. Mrs. Petronia wore a paint-splattered shirt
over leggings and high-top sneakers. "We left the boys
at home with a babysitter," she explained with a smile.
"Somehow, we didn't think they'd be very helpful with
this project."

Maddy arrived with her parents, whom I'd never
seen wearing anything other than dressy work clothes.
But today, they both wore old jeans and shirts, and
Mrs. Eaton's hair was covered with a red bandanna.

Grandpa didn't seem to know quite what to do
with himself or with all of these people in his bakery.
Grandma had set out pastries, milk, and coffee for
everyone. They busied themselves cleaning countertops
and watching us, but they reminded me of two ants
whose anthill had just been invaded.

Before we got started, Ella, Maddy, and I explained
our plan to create an inviting feeling at First Street
Family Bakery with bright colors and a few small tables
and chairs, inside and out.

"Of course," I said, "it won't work for people to sit

outside in the winter. But for three seasons out of the year, they could!"

Mrs. Eaton beamed. "We have a good assortment of furniture in our warehouse," she said. "Some pieces sit there for years and never make it to our antique shop. I told the girls that we may have exactly the tables and chairs they're looking for."

Grandpa cleared his throat and said, "I'm afraid we can't afford to spend a lot of money." The Eatons' antique store is known for being super expensive.

Mr. Eaton leveled his serious gaze at Grandpa. "I have loved this bakery for as long as I can remember," he said. "I want to donate some furniture to the cause."

Grandpa, who must have been holding his breath, seemed to exhale with relief. "That's quite a generous offer," he said.

"Yes, that's very kind, Mr. Eaton," Grandma agreed.

Then Mrs. Petronia added, "We have a few vintage tablecloths. They're sitting in a cupboard, not being used. I think they might be just what you need."

I nodded excitedly. We hadn't even lifted a paint-brush yet, and already I was convinced that we could make this work.

A Painting Party

Josh and his friends set up ladders outside and started cleaning the exterior of the bakery storefront. He had promised his friends a lunch of sloppy joes, potato chips, and lots of freshly baked desserts. They must have been hungry, because by late morning, some of them were already putting on the first coats of new paint.

It was no surprise that Maddy had a great eye for color. "Pink Icing there," she said, pointing to the window trim, "but not there. We want the colors to pop!"

A warm breeze blew dried leaves along the sidewalk as I stood outside with Dad, admiring our progress.

"Incredible," Dad said. "The paint really freshens it up. You guys are good!"

Josh craned his neck from the top of his ladder and looked down. "Wait until we paint the frame around the windows. Maddy was thinking of using two colors."

"I like how she thinks," Dad said.

I gave Maddy a thumbs-up. She was doing exactly what she loved, and she was *good* at it, too.

While one crew worked outside, the rest of us worked inside to transform the front of the shop. We covered the counters and display cases with plastic tarps, washed down the walls and trim, and started painting. Before long, the dull and faded walls and woodwork looked brighter and fresher.

As I waited for Mom to pour more blue paint into my pan, I looked around at the Cherry Red shelves and the Powder Blue walls. Behind the service counter, Mrs. Petronia was trimming the mirror with Pink Icing, and Mr. P. was adding the same color to the trim around the doors and windows. It looked as if a whole new business was starting up here!

I knew my own business also needed tending to—orders were piling up. But my friends and I had decided that this weekend, we needed to focus on the town's oldest and finest bakery. We took just enough time to reply to our customers' orders online. We told them that we were taking the weekend off but would get back to them very soon.

And then, I remembered something. "Mr. P.!" I asked suddenly. "Did you get that job you were hoping to hear about a week or two ago?"

Everybody stopped working and waited for his answer.

He drew a deep breath and slowly shook his head.

"It just wasn't meant to be," he said. "It looks like you girls are stuck with me just a little bit longer."

"Good!" I exclaimed. "I mean, not good that you didn't get the job."

"But good for us," Maddy said, pausing from sweeping.

Ella glanced over from the back wall, where she was spackling over nail holes. She didn't say anything.

"That means I have time to tend chickens and get more fresh eggs to you girls," Mr. P. said with a laugh. "And I have to admit, I have way more fun helping with your baking than working in an office."

I nodded and gave him a warm smile. I was sad for him that the job hadn't worked out, but so glad for us that we could keep him for a while longer!

Then I pulled out my phone to snap a few photos of the new and improved bakery.

I knew that Sylvie would love to see how—with her design suggestions and everyone's efforts—we were transforming the old bakery into something really special.

Click! Click! Click!

By the end of the day on Sunday, the smell of paint was still in my nostrils. But we'd done it. The entry door, the walls—inside and out—and every bit of trim around windows and along the ceiling and floor were freshly painted. And Mr. and Mrs. Eaton had brought in some cute little bistro tables and chairs, too, from their warehouse.

The finishing touch? Little glass vases. I used some of the money from my LPP profits to buy them. There were always vases of flowers on the tables in all the photos Sylvie had sent. It was the perfect detail to make First Street Family Bakery look like an authentic French *pâtisserie*. Grandma promised to add fresh flowers to the vases in the morning.

"Now all we have to do is let the paint dry," Mr. Eaton said as we cleaned up in the back kitchen.

Before we left, my friends and I made new signs for our bakery cart. Then we rolled it outside and set it beside the front door of the bakery, using one of Josh's bike locks to secure the cart to a bike rack. The signs proclaimed:

A Painting Party

"A FRESH NEW LOOK!"
"COME CHECK US OUT!"
"TIME FOR TREATS!"

It was almost seven o'clock when all three of our families, plus Grandma and Grandpa, were crowded around tables pushed together at Da Vinci's, my favorite Italian restaurant.

When our dinners arrived, I showered my plate of spaghetti and meatballs with Parmesan cheese. The last time I'd had this meal, when Mom and Dad had been trying to convince me to "accept what was," I was feeling *hopeless*. Tonight, as I looked around at our big table, I was amazed at all we'd accomplished together. I was definitely feeling *hopeful* now.

Grandpa pushed his chair back from the table and stood up, holding his glass of water. He was going to make a toast. I'd seen him do this once before—at Aunt Sophie and Uncle Bernard's wedding reception.

He cleared his throat. "We want to thank everyone for your help in giving First Street Family Bakery a brand-new look—and maybe a brand-new start. It all looks a little girly to me—"

Everyone laughed. Grandpa winked at me, and then smiled at Ella and Maddy.

"—but my granddaughter and her friends tell me that these changes are going to bring in more customers. I sure hope you girls are right," Grandpa said as he raised his glass. "Cheers!"

"Cheers!" everyone repeated, lifting and clinking their glasses.

I joined in, lifting my glass of milk and clinking it with Ella's and Maddy's glasses and then with Grandma's and Grandpa's glasses. I was happy at that moment. Whatever happened next, we had all done our best to keep our businesses going.

Destiny
Chapter 11

I could barely sit still at my desk on Monday, wondering how customers would view the renovated bakery, now that it was open again.

As I left Mr. Bauer's classroom for the day, he followed me into the hallway. "Hey, Grace," he said as other students poured past, "your baking business must really be taking off!"

I wasn't sure what he meant by that. With all the work we'd put into First Street Family Bakery over the last week, my friends and I were way behind on checking our orders for *La Petite Pâtisserie*. We were going to have some serious catching up to do this week.

I must have given Mr. Bauer a confused look, because he added, "Someone said you girls took over the old First Street Family Bakery space."

Huh? "Well, um, we've been using the kitchen

there . . ." I started to explain, but then another teacher stopped beside us and started asking Mr. Bauer about the school-wide testing we'd have next week.

While Mom drove us to the bakery, I tried to fill in Ella and Maddy on what had just happened. "What if Grandma and Grandpa hear those rumors?" I asked Mom. "What if they think we're trying to take over their bakery?"

Mom laughed. "I heard those rumors, too," she said. "People jump to conclusions sometimes before they know the facts. Don't worry about it, Grace. Your grandparents know it isn't true."

I hoped she was right. But when she dropped us off in front of the bakery, my worry melted away. The storefront, with its new paint and trim, sparkled.

For just a moment, my friends and I stood outside. "I love the way it looks," Ella said, her hands pressed to her lips.

"It's awesome," Maddy agreed.

I agreed. Everything about the bakery, right down to the window boxes filled with pine boughs, said, "Something new is happening here! Come check us out."

Destiny

Even though the red "For Sale" sign was still in the window, it blended in with the surrounding red paint and looked a little less noticeable. With the bloom of new colors, I hoped no one would see it at all.

"Hello, girls!" Grandma said as we stepped through the front door. She was wearing a brand-new apron with the same reds, light blues, and pinks of the bakery color scheme. She matched the new decor!

Grandma noticed our eyes on her apron. "I was inspired," she said, "and took time to sew it for myself last night."

I couldn't help but smile.

Across from the service counter sat three small round tables, each with two chairs. And on top of vintage tablecloths, the little glass vases each held one red rose. I almost wanted to cry. Together, we'd worked a miracle!

The swinging door from the kitchen opened, and Grandpa came out, calling, "Hey-ya, girls!" Then he pretended to be blinded by the bright new paint colors. He blocked his eyes with his arm.

"Oh, Grandpa," I said. "I bet you secretly love it."

Grandma laughed. "I think he actually does,

Grace!" she said, wrapping me in a big hug.

When a handful of customers came in the front door, my friends and I sat down at a table to eavesdrop on their reactions.

One couple said, "We just had to see what's going on here. What a sweet little bakery!"

Another woman said, "I love the colors!"

After they left, each with a purchase, Grandma said to us, "You wouldn't believe how many new customers we've had today—people who've never stepped foot in here before."

"Plus," Grandpa added, "we had two people ask about the 'For Sale' sign out front."

I cringed. "But that's not why we redecorated," I protested. "We're trying to save the bakery, not sell it."

"I know, I know," Grandpa said. "Sorry if I upset you, Grace. But we need to be realistic. A few more customers this month may not be enough to solve our financial challenges." Then he nodded toward the kitchen. "Mr. P.'s in back. He's already checking your website for orders. Sounds like you girls are going to be pretty busy this week!"

As we headed to the kitchen, the front door chimed,

announcing another customer. Or a possible buyer. I glanced back, and then I stopped. The woman stepping into the bakery looked *so* familiar. I knew her from somewhere, but I just couldn't place her.

"Afternoon, ma'am," the woman said to Grandma in a thick southern accent. That's when I realized she was the porter from the train! What was her name? Destiny? She had been so nice to me when she brought my birthday cake to the table in the dining car. After we'd told her about LPP, she'd told us she liked to bake, too.

I turned back to the kitchen and was through the swinging door when I heard Destiny say, "I was so excited when I saw your sign!"

Wait. The For Sale sign? Is she excited about buying the bakery?

I turned around as fast as I could, pushed the swinging door open a crack, and peered out. Destiny was sitting down at one of the small tables, motioning for Grandma and Grandpa to join her. As I watched, she pulled a few sheets of paper out of her purse. I tried to hear what they were saying, but the clatter of dishes from the kitchen covered their voices.

"Grace, come on," Ella called.

"We've got work to do," Maddy added.

Stomach clenched, I let the door close softly. I couldn't shake the feeling that Destiny was going to buy Grandma and Grandpa's business. I couldn't bear to say anything to Maddy, Ella, or Mr. P. I really just wanted to go home and crawl under the covers. But I couldn't. I still had my own business to run. I tried to put Destiny—and the awful feeling in my stomach—out of my mind.

Luckily there was enough work with LPP to keep me focused on other things. While we'd been busy giving First Street Family Bakery a face-lift, a flurry of orders for *La Petite Pâtisserie* had piled up. And within the customer comments for those orders, the rumors were definitely flying:

So exciting to see your little business take off!

Love the new paint on the old bakery! Exciting!

We'll miss the old bakery, but this is good news for you girls!

⌐ Destiny ⌐

I turned away from Mr. P.'s laptop. "I wish people would quit saying that!" I said in frustration. "We're not taking over the bakery."

"I know," said Mr. P. "They're just not sure what to make of the changes. It'll all sort itself out."

Ella handed me a marker, and we began transferring each order to our whiteboard.

When Grandma and Grandpa stepped into the kitchen, I couldn't look at them. I was worried that they had just found a buyer for their business—all because we'd made the bakery look so good. Wouldn't that be a joke on us? I forced my lips shut. If I wasn't careful, I might say something to hurt someone's feelings.

Instead, I carefully wrote the last order on our whiteboard. Then I crossed my arms and stared at it. It was so full!

Maddy exhaled hard. "The orders have been coming in a lot faster lately. How can we possibly handle all of them?"

"I don't know," Ella said. "We used to get just a few orders each week. But now people are placing them way ahead—even for the holidays."

Will we be baking here at the holidays? I wondered. *Or*

will someone else own the bakery by then?

"Whoa, here's an order from Illinois," said Mr. P. in disbelief. "That's one we won't be able to fill. I don't think we're licensed to ship goods to other states."

"Oh dear," said Grandma, peering at the computer. "You're right—you'll need a wholesale license for that. We have one, though we rarely get orders from out of state."

"How on earth did they learn about LPP?" Grandpa asked from the doorway.

"The website—and maybe the blog," Maddy explained. "Things can really take off with that kind of advertising."

Grandpa grunted. I finally glanced up at him. He looked at Grandma and then nodded slightly in my direction. What were my grandparents thinking? Did they have something to tell me about their conversation with Destiny? I braced myself for the news.

Instead, Grandma removed her newly sewn apron and walked to a freshly laundered stack of plain white aprons. She grabbed two—one for herself, and one for Grandpa. "We just closed up out front," she explained. "We were going to head home, but it's plain as day that you all could use a little extra help."

"Tell us what to do, Grace," Grandpa said, putting on a clean apron. "We don't want to get in the way, but if we can lend a hand, we'd sure like to."

"That would be great!" I said, relieved that neither one of them had mentioned Destiny. "How do you feel about learning a few new recipes?"

"Sounds great," Grandpa said, winking at me. "Change can be good, remember?"

I had to laugh. Grandpa was making the best of things. I would try to do the same. Besides, we had baking to do. That always put me in a good mood. I turned on my tablet, and soon the kitchen was full of French music and busy workers.

Given everything on our whiteboard, which included some orders to fill and deliver by tomorrow, we couldn't possibly be done by dinnertime. "Anyone interested in staying on if we turn this into a pizza party?" I asked hopefully.

Ella and Maddy nodded eagerly, and even Grandma and Grandpa agreed. I made a call home.

"Mom?" I asked. "Do you think you and Dad could bring pizza here so that we can keep working? We have so much to do, and Grandma and Grandpa are helping, too."

She agreed, thank goodness. Before I put my phone away, I took a group selfie of me, my grandparents, my friends, and Mr. P. in the kitchen—up to our elbows in orders! We were busy, but everyone was having fun.

Click!

The night before Thanksgiving, scents of sautéed garlic, onion, and celery filled the kitchen. I sat cross-legged in the bay window with my tablet in hand and Bonbon settled in beside me. Mom and Dad were both at the stove, making stuffing and cranberry sauce for tomorrow's turkey dinner.

After posting the photo of our pizza party at the bakery, I was trying to write a Thanksgiving entry to go with it. I'd been so worried about my grandparents' business lately, but I also had a lot to be grateful for today—like how far my own business had come and the way everyone had always pitched in to help us.

I didn't know quite how to put my feelings into

words, but finally, I drew a deep breath and simply started typing:

Like many businesses, La Petite Pâtisserie will be closed on Thanksgiving Day.

We want to spend time with our families—and what great families we have!!!

Following our dream hasn't always been easy, but we've always felt our families' love. So this holiday, we want to give a big shout-out of thanks.

Thank you to my mom and dad for letting us use their kitchen when we first started our business. We know that wasn't always easy—and was sometimes really messy. :)

Thank you to my brother Josh for helping to build us a beautiful bakery cart.

Thank you to Maddy's parents for helping us start our own website.

Thank you to Ella's parents, especially Mr. P.—who helps us in some way almost every day.

A big thank-you to my French relatives—Aunt Sophie, Uncle Bernard, and my cousins Sylvie and Lily—for teaching me about French baking and inspiring me to start LPP.

And Grandma and Grandpa? How can I thank you enough? Thank you for believing in me and for teaching us so much about running our own business. And for letting us use your bakery's kitchen. You're the best!

I felt a lump rise in my throat. When I thought about that bakery being sold out from under us, I didn't know what to write—or even what to think. *Accept what is,* Dad always says. Could I? And could I find a way to be grateful even if things didn't go my way?

I took another deep breath, and then typed a few more words:

I don't know what the future will bring, but I am so grateful for everything that has happened so far—and for all the people who have helped us along the way. Merci beaucoup!

Early the next week, everything changed.

On Monday afternoon, as we were putting on our aprons, Grandpa called to us from the doorway of the kitchen. "Girls, can you come out front for a moment? Mr. P.—you, too. There's someone who wants to talk to you."

Before the door swung shut, I caught a glimpse of that someone standing at the bakery counter.

Destiny.

My stomach clenched.

This was it. We were getting the news. The bakery had a buyer, and that spelled the end for LPP. *Accept what is,* I reminded myself as I filed out of the kitchen behind Ella and Maddy. *Accept what is.*

Destiny stood in front of the counter holding a stack of papers—and a brochure from *La Petite Pâtisserie*.

"I'd like to place an order," Destiny said, waving the brochure in our direction. I could see that several items were circled, and there were notes in the margins.

"I was so impressed by you girls and your French pastry business when we met on the train a while back," Destiny explained. "Y'all stuck in my head. But for the life of me, I couldn't remember the name or the website. Then last week I saw the sign for First Street Family Bakery, and that's how I found you!"

I blinked.

"You want to buy *treats*?" I repeated. *Not the bakery?* I thought to myself.

"Yes, darlin'," said Destiny with a smile. "Hundreds of kids take the Winter Magic Express—the holiday train ride—the last three Saturdays in December. The treats will be part of the price of the ticket. When the ride ends at the depot, just a block away, we'll lead groups of children here for some hot chocolate and some of those delicious French *pâtisserie* items you girls are bakin'. It will make the holiday ride extra special."

I stared at her with my mouth open—I couldn't help it. I was stunned!

Ella went over the price list with Destiny, and then Maddy wrote the order. The whole time Destiny was talking, my mind was racing. Did this mean Grandma and Grandpa *weren't* selling the bakery?

I leaned close to Grandma and whispered, "I thought Destiny wanted to buy the bakery."

Destiny

Grandma looked confused. "No—heavens no." She whispered back. "What gave you that idea?"

"Last week I heard her tell you and Grandpa that she saw the sign," I explained quietly. "I thought she meant the For Sale sign."

Grandma shook her head. "Destiny only wants to buy pastries," Grandma reassured me. "Not a whole bakery. You girls were so busy that day that Grandpa and I gave her one of your brochures and asked her to come back today to place her order."

I suddenly felt a pang of guilt. Destiny could be ordering treats from First Street Family Bakery instead. "Grandma, I don't want to take business away from you and Grandpa!"

"It's okay, sweetheart," Grandma said. "We're going to provide the hot chocolate. Besides, all those parents are bound to want coffee. We'll sell that."

All those parents. That's when it finally hit me. *Hundreds* of kids. Train rides *three* weekends in a row.

Destiny left, and I looked at Ella and Maddy, who were both looking at me.

"Um, Grace?" Maddy said. "This is a really big order."

"Can we bake this much?" Ella asked.

"Are there enough hours in the week?" Maddy added. "And what about our other orders?"

Mr. P. read the order, and even he looked concerned. "We may need to hire another part-time helper to help out *this* part-timer," he joked.

I tried not to feel overwhelmed. This was *good* news, after all. The bakery wasn't being sold—at least not yet. And our business was more successful than ever. But we needed more help!

Grandma gave me a hug. "What problems we have, eh, Grace?" she said with a smile. "You girls have more orders than you can fill, and not enough time to fill them. Your grandpa and I have plenty of time, but not enough orders!"

I leaned into her hug, wishing I could send some of our orders her way. And then it hit me. *Could I?*

I pulled back and stood up. "We should work to-gether," I announced.

Grandpa nodded. "We're happy to help you girls, whenever you need . . ." he began.

"No, I mean for real—permanently," I said.

Maddy caught on to my idea. "Yes!" she said. "Like

a business partnership—combining our bakery businesses to make them each stronger!"

Even Mr. P. stroked his chin thoughtfully. "It does seem to me that if we work *together*, maybe everyone can benefit," he said. "We have a growing business and a popular menu, but we need more skilled bakers, and a location, and the ability to ship orders to other states." Mr. P. looked at Grandma and Grandpa, a question in his eyes.

Grandpa hesitated. "I don't know about all that. I was just getting used to the idea of retiring sometime soon. Maybe going somewhere warm for a week or two in the winter . . ."

"You could still do that!" Ella spoke up. "My dad could manage the bakery while you're on vacation."

I saw Grandma's eyes light up at that. When was the last time my grandparents had taken a vacation?

Grandma and Grandpa exchanged a look. It was a small gesture, but I knew what it meant. They were considering the idea.

I felt a soft breeze of relief sweep through me.

La Grande Pâtisserie

Chapter 12

When we met again with my grandparents at the bakery on Tuesday night, they asked us to bring our parents along. And they gave us the answer we were hoping for: a big YES.

"There's more," said Grandma. "We would like to officially buy into your business and to pay you—maybe in monthly installments—what you think is a fair price for all you've invested in it already and for the recipes you've created."

I beamed back at them.

Grandma added, "Now don't think this decision is based on how much we love our granddaughter." She gave me a knowing look, and I laughed.

"It's a big decision," Grandpa said. "And we've given it considerable thought. In a short time you girls have managed to build your business and start paying back your investors. That's remarkable."

Grandpa's compliment made me smile. I looked to Ella and Maddy, who were both grinning from ear to ear. We really *had* accomplished something incredible together!

"And because business is picking up, we'll be able to hire Mr. Petronia," said Grandpa, "Part-time at first. Maybe someday soon it will be *full-time*."

Mr. P. dipped his head in appreciation.

"We also want to be sure that no matter how busy this business gets, you girls work less during the school year," added Grandma.

I saw my mom mouth a silent "thank you" to my Grandma. Ella was nodding, too. A little less pressure, without giving up our business, *would* be nice.

"There's one more thing," Grandma added. "With the new look of First Street Family Bakery, we're thinking that maybe it's time for a new name, too. More and more customers are expecting to find your French treats when they step in the door."

I felt like I owed Grandma an apology. "Honest," I said. "We weren't trying to take over your bakery."

"We know that, honey," Grandma said, dismissing

the idea with a wave of her hand. "But it's all working to drive business through this door. It's a big idea, actually."

"You mean a *grande* idea," I said, using the French word for big. "Hey, if you want a new name," I said, "how about *La Grande Pâtisserie*?"

"I love it," Ella and Maddy said in unison.

"Sounds grand!" Grandpa grinned.

Grandma nodded. "It's perfect!" she agreed.

I thought again of the blog we had created for *La Petite Pâtisserie*, and then of our website and all the packaging lining the walls in the back kitchen. "Wait," I said slowly. "What exactly would happen to our business—to *La Petite Pâtisserie*?"

Grandma tilted her head. "I think we just have to come up with creative ways to keep both parts of the business going. Do you have any big ideas, girls?"

Ella chewed her lip. "I have a small idea," she said. "We do have the little bakery cart."

"Yes!" I said. "We could still sell from the cart during the summer months. And use it to advertise bigger sales here at the bakery."

"And bring it out for taste tests and special events,

like the Winter Magic Express train rides," added Ella.

Maddy sat on the edge of her chair, wiggling her legs and feet. "Maybe our website could still be called *La Petite Pâtisserie*," she said thoughtfully, "so that our customers don't get confused. But we could use the website and our blog to advertise special events at our storefront—*La Grande Pâtisserie*—too."

"Lots of great ideas, girls," said Maddy's mom.

"Yes," said Grandpa, the twinkle back in his eyes now. "It looks to me as if everyone agrees we should join forces and work together. Do you want to vote? Those for the idea, raise your hand."

Ella, Maddy, and I shot our hands up high.

"Well, that's easy!" Grandma declared. "A unanimous decision."

I couldn't help but jump up and do a happy dance.

My friends got up and danced beside me, too. The last time we'd been this happy was when . . . well, back when we'd first started to bake in Grandma and Grandpa's kitchen. Back when we were first dreaming of a trip to Paris together.

"Hey, wait!" I announced to my friends. I raced back into the kitchen and toward the metal cabinet in the corner. I opened a drawer, found the wholesale catalogue that held images of Paris, and pulled them out and studied them. Every image was just as I'd remembered it: a white-haired man in a beret, sitting on a park bench, feeding pigeons; the Eiffel Tower lit up at night; and the Seine river, glistening beneath Notre Dame Cathedral.

Grandma found me in the kitchen and saw what I had in my hands. "Well, well. There they are," she said. "I wondered what happened to those pictures. You could put them back up here again, or we could frame a few and put them out front in the customer area."

I smiled at Grandma. She always understands my dreams.

"I'd love that," I said, carefully setting down the images and pulling her into a hug.

Late Thursday afternoon, just before dinner, the phone rang. I was setting the table when I heard Mom say, "Who is this again? The Massachusetts School of Cooking?"

ᴄᴡ La Grande Pâtisserie ᴄᴡ

That's when my heart started fluttering. Probably, it was nothing. Probably, it was just a phone call telling me they'd received my contest entry, but still . . .

Then Mom covered the mouthpiece of the phone and said, "Grace, it's for you. I think it's good news!"

I took the phone, but I could barely understand what the speaker was saying.

A few words popped out at me:

"*Congratulations . . . Your Dreams of Paris recipe . . . thousand dollar check on its way . . .*"

When I hung up the phone, I screamed and jumped into the air.

Poor Bonbon scrabbled inside her crate.

"Mom! Dad! Josh! I won!"

Over dinner, I hogged the whole conversation. I couldn't help myself. I was almost too excited to eat.

I did a quick mental calculation. "Between the money I've saved from our baking business, plus what I just won, I have enough to fly to Paris and visit our French family!"

And then, as soon as the words left my lips, my feelings darkened, as if a heavy drape were pulled across a window. "Oh no. What about Ella and Maddy?

We've talked about going to Paris someday *together*. We're all saving for it. And to make matters worse, they don't even know that I entered the contest."

"Really? Why is that?" Dad asked.

"Because the last we'd talked about the contest, I said I was too busy to enter it," I explained. "We were *all* too busy. Then Maddy and Ella almost quit LPP, and I was down in the dumps. I decided to bake something just to cheer myself up. I didn't think about the contest until *after* I made the dessert."

"It sounds like you're torn about telling your friends, Grace," Mom said. "What's the best solution?"

I shook my head. "I just don't know."

That Saturday morning was unusually warm for December, so Josh invited me to go bike riding before I headed to the bakery. "We haven't ridden together in forever, and this might be our last chance before it snows," he urged. "Besides, I want to make sure the gears are good to go on a bike I just fixed up."

I tucked Bonbon into the bike trailer, and off I

pedaled. It felt good to bike along with my brother.
I followed him down the towpath, across a short
bridge, and onto a bike trail that wound farther out of
Bentwick.

Around us, empty branches seemed to lift up the
gray sky. The air—damp and cool—promised snow
before long.

When Josh stopped at a metal truss bridge, we got
off our bikes and leaned them against the railing.
I wasn't about to leave Bonbon in her trailer. She'd grow
impatient and try to claw free. So I unzipped the mesh
door, unhooked the dog-fastener, and snapped a leash
onto her collar. Then we followed Josh onto the bridge.

"Remember when we came here as little kids?" Josh
asked, gazing at the river below.

I nodded. "We had a picnic with Mom and Dad
over there." I pointed to the slope on the right. "Do you
remember playing catch with a red rubber ball?"

"Yeah," Josh said with a laugh, "until you tossed it
in the river, and the water was flowing too fast for us
to catch it."

"I don't remember that part," I said, grinning.

"I do," Josh insisted. "I remember watching that

ball float farther and farther away, and I remember how badly I wanted to jump in and go after it. But Dad wouldn't let me."

"Parents," I said, with mock grumpiness.

"Yeah, they're always saving us, aren't they?"

It felt good to laugh with Josh. And then, as if watching for that ball, he stared off silently into the river for a long time.

As I watched the river flow between two banks and under the bridge we stood on, I realized something: I am kind of like a bridge, too.

I'd been a bridge between two cultures, French and American.

A bridge between my grandparents' old ways of doing business and new ideas.

A bridge between my grandparents here and Sylvie back in France.

And then my decision came to me.

"Josh, what if I buy a ticket for Sylvie to come here? She gave us so many great ideas for the bakery's make-over. I could show her everything we've done." The more I talked, the more excited I became. "I know Maddy and Ella would love to meet Sylvie in person.

And she could get to know Grandma and Grandpa better, too!"

Josh smiled. "Makes sense to me," he said.

"My friends and I can still save for a trip to Paris someday," I continued, thinking out loud. "It will be easier to tell them that I won the contest when I tell them that I'm using the prize money to fly Sylvie to the States."

In fact, now that the bakery business was good— for Grandma and Grandpa *and* for my friends and me—I couldn't think of anything that I wanted more than to have Sylvie here. I bent down and hugged Bonbon. *She* would be glad to see Sylvie, too!

The Winter Magic Express
Chapter 13

*A*s each day passed, I felt lighter—happier than ever. It felt amazingly good to build an even bigger French *pâtisserie* business in the bakery I loved, with Grandma and Grandpa by my side. Sylvie and Aunt Sophie sent us some of their favorite recipes, and we learned how to create a whole new assortment of French baked goods. And with guidance from Mrs. Eaton, we expanded our website to include an advertising section for *La Grande Pâtisserie,* too.

When the second Saturday in December came, things got really busy. As planned, at three-thirty p.m., the Winter Magic Express train ride ended with treats and hot chocolate at *La Grande Pâtisserie.* Countless kids and their parents poured off the train, hustled to the bakery, and fluttered in like a flock of hungry birds, leaving nothing but crumbs behind.

Grandma and Grandpa served hot chocolate, coffee, and hot apple cider from the counter. Maddy and Ella and I handed out treats from our bakery cart, which we'd decorated with sprigs of holly and silver bells.

"What just hit us?" Grandma said after the last family left. "I've never seen such a commotion!"

But she was smiling, and my friends and I were, too. Business was good!

When the next Saturday came, we started getting ready for the Winter Magic Express crowd even earlier, for two reasons. First, we now knew how much work it was. The rush of customers meant "all hands on deck." We even asked Josh if he could help at the counter that afternoon, too.

The *other* reason we prepared early was because today was a doubly special day: Sylvie would arrive this afternoon! Even though we had been video-chatting, I couldn't wait to see her again. I was so excited to show her *La Grande Pâtisserie.* Sylvie and I were going to bake together, just like we had in Paris. But this time, our grandparents and my friends would be with us.

Maddy and Ella and I spent the morning putting the finishing touches on the treats for the kids from the train. Then we stocked the baking cart, which was set up near the entry door. As we worked, my friends kept catching my eye and smiling. I could tell they were excited to finally meet Sylvie in person. They had even forgiven me for entering the online baking contest without them, once they learned that I'd spent the winnings on a plane ticket for Sylvie!

When everything was ready, I ducked into the bathroom and changed from my jeans into the dress I'd bought just for today. I smoothed the velvet waistband of the pink skirt and adjusted my headband. It had a little fan of pink tulle on it, which I thought looked very French. I hoped Sylvie would think so, too!

"Grandma and Grandpa," I said, as Maddy and Ella and I put on our coats. "Are you sure you don't want to come with us to pick up Sylvie?"

Grandpa shook his head. "Wish we could, Grace, but things are hoppin' here," he said, waving his hand at the customers in line and lingering at tables. "We'll be here when you get back."

Then my friends and I piled into my mom's minivan and headed to Logan International Airport in Boston to meet Sylvie. It was finally time!

Passengers on international flights have to go through customs and have their passports stamped. I knew from experience that it could take a long time, but that didn't make waiting any easier.

Eventually—finally!—a girl with sandy waves of hair appeared, pulling a suitcase with one hand and gripping a small black-and-white stuffed animal to her chest with the other.

"Sylvie!" I called. "We're over here!"

She looked around the crowded lobby and finally spotted the long banner my friends and family held up. It read *"Bonjour,* Sylvie! Welcome to the USA!"

A smile filled Sylvie's face. She squealed and ran toward me, leaving her suitcase behind. "Hello, Grace!"

I rushed forward to greet her. We hugged, and I kissed her on each cheek, just as she had done to me when I arrived in Paris so many months ago.

"What's this?" I asked, pointing to the stuffed dog.

"C'est ma petite chienne, Bonbon," she said with a big smile. "It's my little dog, Bonbon."

Out of the corner of my eye, I saw a woman with a

stroller rolling Sylvie's suitcase to her side. "You might need this while you're visiting."

I spun toward the familiar voice.

"Surprise, Grace!" the woman said.

"Aunt Sophie!" I gave her a hug and then peered into the stroller. "And you brought Lily!"

Lily was much bigger now, and she grinned back at me and babbled something, as if she thought I should clearly understand her. "Oh, I'm glad you're here, too, Lily," I said, kissing her head. "We're going to have so much fun!"

I couldn't believe my French family had surprised me this way. "Mom, did you know?" I asked.

"Of course," she said with a grin as she hugged her sister.

"Grace," Aunt Sophie explained, "since you so generously used your winnings to buy Sylvie's ticket, I dipped into savings and bought a ticket so that I could join the fun," she said. "And Lily flew for free!"

Ella and Maddy were standing off to the side, as if they didn't know what to do. I reached for their hands and drew them closer. Then I stepped toward Sylvie so that we made a small circle.

"We're all finally together," I said happily. "These two," I said, turning to Sylvie, "are my best friends. And this," I said, putting my arm around Sylvie, "is my cousin."

Ella grinned. *"Bonjour,* Sylvie!"

"After video-chatting with you, it's like we're already friends!" Maddy exclaimed.

Sylvie dropped her hands. I hoped she wasn't going to turn super shy and distant, the way she'd acted toward me those first weeks in Paris.

But instead, she leaned forward and kissed my friends' cheeks. Then she patted her chest, where her heart sits, and in her French accent said, "We are good friends."

From that moment, I knew everyone was going to have a wonderful time together.

As we made our way to the parking ramp, Sylvie answered Maddy's and Ella's questions about the flight. She had to pause a few times and ask Aunt Sophie to translate, but I could see that Sylvie wasn't as shy as she'd been when I'd visited her in Paris. But that had been last June, before Lily had been born and just after Sylvie had lost her beloved *grand-mère*. Now, half a year had passed, and so much had happened. I'd grown and changed over that time, and I'd learned a lot. It was clear that Sylvie had, too.

Growing up.

Maybe it's all about becoming who you truly are, a little more every day.

When we made it back to Bentwick, we stopped at home to drop off the luggage and let Aunt Sophie and Sylvie freshen up. Baby Lily didn't care. She was sound asleep.

Bonbon ran up to us the moment we entered the house. Sylvie grinned and sank to her knees right there in the hallway. "Bonbon!" she said, hugging my little dog, who pressed her black nose into Sylvie's palm.

Before I'd even met Bonbon, Sylvie had known her as a stray in Paris and had fed her bits of bread. Mom and I had brought Bonbon home with us. Despite the time that had passed, Bonbon remembered Sylvie! She barked happily and covered Sylvie with wet kisses.

Sylvie stroked Bonbon's head and spoke to her

sweetly in French. I didn't understand most of what she said, except for the word *maison*. Home. I knew Sylvie was happy that Bonbon had a home with me.

Maddy and Ella and I helped Sylvie haul her suitcase upstairs. Sylvie and I were sharing my room, just as we had shared Sylvie's room in Paris. I'd cleared out a dresser drawer for Sylvie to use, just as she'd cleared one for me. In Paris, Sylvie's room was covered with pictures of flowers. I'd filled a vase with fresh flowers and put it on my nightstand. It was one more way to let Sylvie know how glad I was that she was here.

Sylvie noticed the flowers right away, and she *oohed* and *aahed* over the photos I'd taken in Paris and tacked up on my bulletin board. "I love your *chambre*," Sylvie said as the four of us sat on my bed. Mom had reminded me that Sylvie would be tired from the long plane ride, but after washing her face and changing her clothes, Sylvie was wide awake.

Perfect. Our plan would work.

Destiny had given Ella, Maddy, and me free tickets for today's ride on the Winter Magic Express. When I'd explained that my cousin would be arriving from Paris, Destiny added a fourth free ticket. Mom had said we could all go as long as Sylvie wasn't too jet-lagged. When we told Sylvie, her eyes danced with excitement.

"But before that," I added, "we're going to the bakery. Grandma and Grandpa can't wait to see you."

Sylvie jumped up from the bed. "We go now?" she asked eagerly.

The four of us thundered down the steps and into the living room. Mom, holding a still-sleeping Lily, shushed us and started to give us a quiet scolding. But when Sylvie explained that she wanted to go to the bakery, Aunt Sophie looked excited, too. "I can't wait to see how you all transformed First Street Family Bakery into *La Grande Pâtisserie*," she said. *"Allons-y!* Let's go!"

"All right," Mom said. "Everyone back in the van! You too, Lily," she whispered, gently buckling the baby into her car seat.

The moment Mom pulled up in front of *La Grande Pâtisserie*, I could tell that Aunt Sophie was impressed. "I never dreamed," she said. "Grace, the pictures you sent us don't do it justice."

Sylvie admired the window boxes full of holiday greenery. *"C'est magnifique!"*

"Oh yes!" I agreed.

"*Oui, oui!*" Ella joined in.

Maddy hopped out and rushed to open the door of the bakery. "*Everything* about today is magnificent!"

Inside, the bakery sparkled with new life. Framed images of Paris popped against the freshly painted walls. The glass display cases brimmed with French treats of every size and color—including Dreams of Paris, my winning recipe. There was even French music in the background, except that it wasn't a CD. Grandma and Grandpa must have hired a musician, because there, in the corner, sitting on a tall stool, playing a red-and-white accordion, was . . . my brother?

"Josh?" Aunt Sophie and I said at the same time. Josh grinned from ear to ear as he played a simple melody and pumped the bellows in and out.

"I knew you were a great pianist," Aunt Sophie said, ruffling Josh's hair. "But I didn't know you could play the accordion."

"Me either," I said. "This day is full of surprises."

Josh put down the bulky instrument and gave Aunt Sophie a hug. "The Eatons had an old one in their antique shop, and they're letting me borrow it," he explained. "But I need more practice." Then he turned to Sylvie and grinned. "Welcome to the best French bakery in Bentwick!"

Sylvie blushed shyly and said a quiet hello, but her words were lost over Grandma's happy greeting.

"Sophie! Sylvie! Lily! Our girls are finally here!" Grandma cried as she rushed from the kitchen wearing her red *pâtisserie* apron.

Grandpa was right behind her. I smiled to see him wearing a bright red tie. *"BonJOUR!"* he called, his French heavy with an American accent. Ella and Maddy and I giggled.

There was a flurry of hugs and hellos as everyone started talking at once. Lily woke up, but Grandpa scooped her into his arms and had her smiling and cooing in no time.

Grandma had her arms wrapped around Sylvie. "Oh, dear Sylvie," she said. "We're so happy you're here. We can finally bake together. And I know you like flowers, so we can go to the botanical gardens. They have a beautiful indoor exhibit of tropical plants, so we'll stay nice and warm, and then—"

"Mom!" Aunt Sophie interrupted, laughing. "Slow down. We just got here."

Grandma smiled. "Oh, I know. We just have a lot of catching up to do with Sylvie." Grandma unwrapped Sylvie from her hug hold and reached for Aunt Sophie. "And that goes for you and Lily, too."

While Grandma gave Aunt Sophie another hug, Sylvie leaned into me. "It is nice," she said with a soft sigh, "our grandparents."

I squeezed Sylvie's hand. I knew she would always miss her French *grand-mère*, but I hoped it would help to know how much her American family loved her.

"Sylvie," Grandpa said, bouncing Lily on his knee. "I understand that we owe much of the new design of the bakery to you. Thank you for all your help!"

Sylvie smiled uncertainly, and I was afraid she didn't understand what he was saying.

I decided she needed a translator—a bridge. I swept my arm out toward the walls of the bakery. "*Grand-père* says *merci*."

"You're welcome," Sylvie replied, smiling proudly.

Snowflakes fell in perfect crystals outside the window as the Winter Magic Express rolled and swayed along the railroad tracks. As we rode past the Blackstone River and through the mill towns, I told Sylvie that some of the buildings were more than two hundred years old. "Grandpa will tell you all about them," I said, rolling my eyes at Maddy and Ella.

Sylvie loved the ride—especially the snow-covered bridges—and Ella and Maddy loved asking Sylvie about Paris, her parents' bakery, and her cat, Napoléon. Sometimes I had to translate, and sometimes I couldn't understand Sylvie's French, either. But that didn't slow us down.

Maddy asked Sylvie what winter was like in Paris, which launched a flurry of questions about celebrating the holidays.

"How do you say 'Merry Christmas' in French?" Ella asked.

"*Joyeux Noël*," Sylvie replied with a smile.

"How do you say 'Happy Hanukkah' in French?" Maddy added.

"*Joyeux Hanoucca*," Sylvie said, pronouncing the words clearly.

"And 'good friends'?" I motioned to all of us. "How do you say, 'We are friends'?"

Sylvie nodded. *"Nous sommes amies!"*

We repeated it together after her.

When the train rolled toward the depot, we were surprised that the ride was over. We'd been so busy talking that we hadn't noticed the time.

Maddy and Ella jumped up and moved toward the doors. Sylvie and I followed. We were going to hurry back to *La Grande Pâtisserie* before the train crowd arrived. "We're serving mini cream puffs," I explained to Sylvie. "Along with *madeleines,* chocolate *tartes,* and red, pink, and green *macarons.*"

"Can I help, too, Grace?" Sylvie asked.

"Bien sûr," I said.

The train braked and squeaked to a stop. As the four of us tumbled out of the car and linked arms, I asked, "Sylvie, how do you say, 'Good food! Let's eat'?"

Everyone knew the answer. We said it together, without missing a beat.

"Bon appétit!"

Glossary of French Words

allons-y *(ah-lohn-zee)*—let's go

baguette *(bah-get)*—a long, thin loaf of French bread

bien sûr *(byen sewr)*—of course

bleu clair *(bluh klehr)*—light blue

bon appétit *(bohn ah-pay-tee)*—good appetite; enjoy your meal

bonbon au chocolat *(bohn-bohn oh sho-ko-lah)*—candy with a soft center and a chocolate outer shell

bonjour *(bohn-zhoor)*—hello

C'est génial! *(say zheh-nyahl)*—That's great!

C'est ma petite chienne, Bonbon. *(say ma puh-teet shyen bohn-bohn)*—It's my little dog, Bonbon.

C'est magnifique! *(say mah-nyee-feek)*—It's beautiful; it's magnificent!

Comment va ta famille? *(koh-mahn vah tah fah-meey)*—How is your family?

Comment vas-tu? *(koh-mahn vah-tew)*—How are you?

et *(ay)*—and

gland *(glahn)*—a pastry filled with sweet custard and decorated with black-and-white frosting

grande pâtisserie *(grahnd pah-tee-suh-ree)*—big bakery

grand-mère *(grahn-mehr)*—grandmother

grand-père *(grahn-pehr)*—grandfather

je ne sais quoi *(zhun say kwah)*—a special quality that cannot be described easily

Je serai ta consultante. *(zhuh suh-ray tah kohn-syewl-tahnt)*—I will be your consultant.

Je t'aime. *(zhuh tem)*—I love you.

Je vais bien. *(zhuh vay byehn)*—I am fine.

Joyeux Hanoucca *(zhwah-yuh ah-noo-kuh)*—Happy Hanukkah

Joyeux Noël *(zhwah-yuh noh-el)*—Merry Christmas

la, le *(lah, luh)*—the

macaron *(mah-kah-rohn)*—a double-layer round cookie that comes in all kinds of colors and flavors

madeleine *(mahd-lehn)*—a small, rich cake baked in a shell-shaped mold

magnifique *(mah-nyee-feek)*—magnificent

mais oui *(meh wee)*—but yes

maison *(meh-zohn)*—home

merci *(mehr-see)*—thank you

merci beaucoup *(mehr-see boh-koo)*—thank you very much

moi *(mwah)*—me

Montmartre *(mohn-mahr-truh)*—a hill in the north of Paris and the district that surrounds it

Napoléon *(nah-poh-lay-ohn)*—the ruler of France after the French Revolution

non *(nohn)*—no

Nous sommes amies. *(noo sumz ah-mee)*—We're friends.

nouvelle *(noo-vel)*—new

oui *(wee)*—yes

Pardonne-moi. *(par-dohn mwah)*—Pardon me; excuse me.

pâtisserie *(pah-tee-suh-ree)*—a French bakery that specializes in pastries and desserts

petite pâtisserie *(puh-teet pah-tee-suh-ree)*—little bakery

religieuse *(ruh-lee-zhyuhz)*—a fancy layered dessert with vanilla and chocolate icing

rose *(rohz)*—pink

rouge *(roozh)*—red

tarte *(tahrt)*—an open-faced pastry shell filled with fruit or custard

tartelette *(tahrt-let)*—a small *tarte*

About the Author

Mary Casanova is always full of ideas. The author of over 30 books—including *Cécile: Gates of Gold, Jess, Chrissa, Chrissa Stands Strong, McKenna*, and *McKenna, Ready to Fly!*—she often travels as far away as Norway, Belize, and France for research.

For *Grace*, she returned to Paris—this time together with her grown daughter, Kate—to bike, explore, and take a French baking class. Mary comes from a long line of bakers. Her grandmothers baked fragrant breads; her mother made the "world's best" caramel rolls and cinnamon rolls; and Mary, too, loves baking breads, cakes, and cookies.

When she's not writing—or traveling for research or to speak at schools and conferences—she's likely reading a good book, horseback riding in the northwoods of Minnesota, or hiking with her husband and three dogs.